Horizon Dynasty

Horizon Crossover Series
(Book III)

by
Lyndi Alexander

Science Fiction Novel from
Dragonfly Publishing, Inc.

HORIZON DYNASTY
Horizon Crossover Series (Book III)
Science Fiction

Hardback Edition
EAN 978-1-941278-00-0
ISBN 1-941278-00-0

Paperback Edition
EAN 978-1-941278-01-7
ISBN 1-941278-01-9

eBook Edition
EAN 978-1-941278-02-4
ISBN 1-941278-02-7

Published in the United States of America by
Dragonfly Publishing, Inc.
www.dragonflypubs.com

ACKNOWLEDGMENTS

Baskets of thanks to my beta readers, Hank Henley, Todd Main, Kellie Hicks and Eric Mountjoy. Your participation in this story is valuable beyond price.

A special thanks to Cynthia Burton, who helped me puzzle out a particularly tricky conundrum.

Thanks also to my editor, Glenda, and publisher Terri, for believing in this story and seeing it through to the end.

DEDICATION

For all those who create their family not by blood or marriage, but through common cause and mutual devotion.

CHAPTER 1

HIDING in the shadows of the tall white brick building on a suburban street in the city of Primor'e, Temms Rogers and his four-member team waited for the signal to move. The light from Terza's second moon faded as it slipped below the horizon, settling the darkness in around them.

It was risky to attack an Agency outpost. But it had been a risk for the Agency to capture Temms' people, loyal members of his *Doubtful* crew, working on the Ancients' space station. One that wasn't going to pay off, if Temms had anything to say about it. He might not be able yet to rescue them, but he certainly intended to make the Agency take notice of him.

A light blinked across the street, at the corner of another old building. Once. Twice. Then twice more. Time to go.

"Tabio," he murmured.

A rustle behind him, then something muscular brushed his arm as it passed unseen. Temms watched the two guards standing in front of the building where he hid. First one, then the second, flailed and fell, their throats torn out by their invisible attacker.

Temms hesitated only long enough to spot *Fuego* captain C.T. Dutton and his four companions sprint across the street to the front steps of the Agency building, before he took his own team around the back. Shapeshifter Tabio, a scaly, efficient assassin clearing the way with his reptilian claws and teeth, would accompany Dutton's team.

Hampered by the absence of two of his best security men and his first officer, all trapped aboard the space station, Temms had chosen the most skilled that he had left. They edged, single file, along the wall, pausing briefly at the corner to assess the security force in the rear of the building. Nothing. Not a man posted.

"Brown?" Temms murmured.

Riviera Brown, a large black woman with a full Afro that made her look even larger, came forward, scanner in one hand, a laser pistol in the other. She leaned out around the corner of the building to inspect the steps, then activated the scanner. The device caught the image of several slow-moving light beams aimed in varying directions from the top of the building to the ground. "Think they be slick, these Agency trash."

Her lazy smile didn't fool Temms. He knew she was sharp as a sword's edge. "Take care of it."

"Yes, sir." Riviera dug in her pack and pulled out two fist-sized devices. She activated the smoke bombs, then tossed them toward the rear of the small yard behind the building. As expected, the light beams flicked in the direction of movement. "We're clear, Captain."

"Got the explosive?"

"Right here, sir."

"Go."

The four scampered along the building to the door. Standing with his back to the wall, Temms watched for defenders from the sides while Riviera and one of the others slapped an incendiary device and detonator on the door lock. "Clear," she said.

They all ducked down, faces turned away. The handle blew with a large *pop*, knocking the door askew on its hinges. Temms kicked it open and they raced inside.

An explosion above rattled the windows around them. "Remember, we're after destruction of things, not people." When the acknowledged his orders, he sent two men armed with a sack full of grenades through the basement, and then took Riviera up to the first floor to rendezvous with Dutton.

Another explosion greeted them as they exited the stairwell, a spray of shattered glass spreading across the fine carpet to their left. In the rooms he passed, polished antique furniture was overturned, upended, even splintered. Acrid smoke filled the air, and intermittent flames popped up, crackling as they devoured the expensive trappings of the Agency offices.

Delcin did say that his officers lived in an atmosphere of superior quality. Funny, their possessions burn just like those real people own.

The demolition filled his heart with precious vindication. The Agency had hurt him. He was giving it back full force. This entire operation was intended to take less than fifteen minutes, its purpose what they used to call "shock and awe" back in his Confederation days.

At the same time, he wasn't a monster. He and Dutton had purposely chosen the time of the attack to be one when the least number of Agency minions would be in the building, and the likelihood that passersby could get caught up in the carnage would be smallest. Just one powerful strike, with one message: "Don't screw with me."

He gestured with his left hand, sending Riviera down the hallway in that direction. He continued into the lobby, where a few blue-uniformed Agency clericals scattered in panic, trying to avoid the black-clothed, masked intruders.

A noise overhead made him glance up. Dutton had climbed onto the balcony over the lobby, and he gave Temms a grin and a thumbs-up before he cut down the large Agency flag with its black field and seven red stars. It gracefully rippled through the air as it drifted to the floor at Temms' feet. He studied it a moment, thought about the past four weeks that his officers, his son, had been held by the Agency. If he couldn't choke them, he at least had the power to destroy this symbol of their so-called superiority. He slipped a firebomb out of his pack and lit it, dropping it right into the center of that flag.

More explosions went off on the upper and lower floors, nearly in synchronicity. The whole building rocked. It was time.

"Let's go, people! We're finished here!"

The flag blazed up, producing a satisfactory stink as its artificial fibers twisted and sizzled. The guerilla team members came running. Dutton counted them out the front door. The last was Tabio, now shifted into human form, an olive-skinned endomorph with straight-cut black hair.

"Got 'em all," Dutton called.

"Clear," Temms replied. He took off the black mask he'd worn and looked directly into the security camera overhead, pointing one accusing finger. Then he followed the others out.

A few curious strangers watched the fires from doorways across the street as the group left the building. Following the plan, the group quickly split up into teams of two, taking separate streets away from the scene of their crime. It was one thing to make a point of showing the Agency who'd trashed their offices, and quite another to get snatched up by local law enforcement.

Temms had Dutton as his assigned companion. Rather than running away, they walked at a measured pace, as if they had a purpose, some place to be. Several blocks away, they entered a small, empty warehouse they'd commandeered for the night. Inside, they'd stocked street clothes for each of the saboteurs. Temms studied the stack of discarded clothing, guessing about half the teams had passed through so far. After a quick, silent change, he and Dutton moved out the far side of the building, heading to a pre-arranged meeting point just outside the city. The last one through had been directed to destroy all the clothing left in that pile. It would be as though they had never been there.

"Guess they'll answer your hails now," Dutton commented as they strolled at a more leisurely pace down the side street.

A grin on his lips, Temms shrugged, an adrenaline high still coursing through him. "It's like the old story with the mule, my friend. First you need to get his attention."

"You'll have that now."

The two walked along, not encountering anyone. Primor'e wasn't a major city of the Terzan subdivision Prana, but the Agency post here serviced the northeastern quadrant of the planet. Its loss would be felt immediately. The Agency's stonewall response since they moved in to occupy the space station would have to change.

"Right now, I just want my people back."

An emotional shudder ran through him at the thought of the officers he'd sent to the Ancients' secret station to help get it up and running. His first officer, Liang Chao Chen, alien Muuvo brothers Uri and Iov, engineer Benzi Quinn, security officer Nim Williams, security chief Tommy Rogers. Temms didn't even know if any of them were alive or dead.

A brooding silence dragged on. "Still can't believe that Jak Moster beat the Agency," Dutton said, "and ended up on that station. He's a tough old bird."

"Yeah. Yeah, that's kind of amazing."

Jak's presence on the station at the time Temms and the ship *Doubtful*'s crew had been invited there had been a subject of much deep thought since the takeover. Was it too much of a coincidence? Had Jak himself had led the Agency to the station? Sure, on the surface he'd avoided any chance for the Agency to find it, and he'd been all hush-hush when he'd first allowed Temms in.

But then how had the Agency discovered the secret, cloaked station within hours of Temms' arrival?

Still too many questions and not enough answers.

They eventually came to the safe house arranged for them on the outskirts of the city. The windows of the small house, covered by slatted blinds, were dimly lit. Dutton knocked rapidly five times, then two more. The door opened, Riviera Brown taking up nearly the whole entrance as she peered outside.

"Oh, Captain—Captains. You come in now, 'fore trouble starts."

She stepped aside, revealing the others gathered around the small holo player, seated on the poverty-level furniture. The two men entered, and came to join those watching the local news feed, showing the breaking story of their little adventure.

"Damned if that doesn't look like a professional job," Dutton mused, nodding thanks as a young woman put a hot drink into his hand. "We should hire ourselves out for blood and thunder."

Temms said nothing. He watched the views of the fire and explosions as they cycled over and over. So wasteful. But it made him feel better.

Your move, Agent Delcin.

Let my people go.

CHAPTER 2

AFTER the news reports confirmed the building was pretty well gutted, with only a few injuries, the captains prepared the second phase of the plan. If the Agency was looking for culprits, they would surely be watching who took off in a hurry right after the attack.

A few days before, when the shuttles had landed them on the planet, in staggered missions to offset suspicion, they'd also left several small flitter ships in areas near the safe house.

Over the next dayturn, they dispatched two of Dutton's team and two from Rogers' team to find the flitters. The small ships would attract less attention when they took off, and if they scattered in different directions upon takeoff, they'd find even less. The shuttles would pick up the captains and the rest of them in the next few days, after the hubbub had died down.

Though he was exhausted once the adrenaline wore off, Temms couldn't relax. He went from window to window, scanning the street outside. Just because it was quiet, didn't mean the Agency might not be waiting to pounce on them. The close quarters in the safe house meant he patrolled a narrow stretch of the flat brown carpeting the better part of the next afternoon.

C.T. put a hand on his arm. "Temms, stop pacing, already. You're not helping my nerves."

The captain of the *Doubtful* pulled away and kept walking. "My nerves are already shot. I haven't slept in so long that...."

He tried to ignore his burning eyes and muscles stiff from constant tension. The passing weeks since his team had been captured had eaten away at his soul, burning away any equivocation over the state of affairs between himself and the Agency. The economic giant that held a stranglehold on the middle planets of their system had been oppressive in its demands even before the Ancients' station was located.

Afterward, it had been totally beyond tolerance.

"Doesn't matter. Things will change now."

C.T.'s men brought a tray from the small kitchen and set it on the wooden table. A tureen steamed, the salty aroma coming from it making Temms' stomach growl. Something about the blond, broad-shouldered young man with the tray reminded him of someone. But he couldn't put his finger on it.

"Come on, Captain Rogers, surrender your worries for a time. Please, eat," the familiar one said, pulling out a chair for him. "If you don't rest soon, your mind will tear itself apart."

Temms studied the young man, who was dressed in a loose blue shirt and black pants. "Have we met?"

The blond smiled. "In a way."

C.T. chuckled. "I didn't know you hadn't seen Nik in this incarnation."

Maybe Temms was just too tired to think, but he was definitely lost. He let the cooks herd him into a chair at the table. Riviera shoved a cup of hot kaffe into his hand, and he took a long sip. "Nik?"

"You probably remember me as Nikki. I fly with Garrett Rawls."

Temms nearly spit out the mouthful of hot beverage. Swallowing quickly, he burnt his tongue and winced. "Nikki? The cute little—ah…." Resenting the smirk on C.T.'s face, he trailed off. "All right. I *don't* understand."

Riviera took the seat across from her captain and helped herself to the thick sliced white bread along with the hearty cream soup, his bewilderment not taking a bite out of her hunger. "There be plenty in this universe we don't understand, sir."

"I'm Nicholas," the young man said. He took the chair next to Temms, then waited politely for the captains to serve themselves before taking some himself. "I am of the Destachan race. We can assume either the male or female form, depending on those around us, or the needs of the moment."

Bewildered at the thought, Temms just nodded. "Of course."

Nicholas laughed. "It takes people awhile to adjust. That's all right. Take your time."

"Mmm."

Temms took another long drink of his kaffe, and then found himself nodding off. He snapped awake, then looked around to see if anyone had noticed. Seemed like everyone was digging into their food. *Blowing up a building was hungry work.*

He felt his eyes closing again, and struggled to keep them open. *I thought kaffe was supposed to wake you up.*

"Told you he wouldn't go easy," Riviera said.

C.T. finished his soup and leaned back. "Don't worry. It'll happen."

"W-What'll happen?" Temms said, feeling all swimmy. What was going on?

C.T. suddenly sat up straight. "Nik, catch him!"

Just that fast, Temms realized he'd been dosed, then he slipped to the right, disappearing into a huge black hole.

* * *

WHEN he came to, he couldn't open his eyes at first. He let himself lie still until he figured out where he was. Except he couldn't. The smells and sounds weren't familiar, but he wasn't moving. There was no rumble of a ship's engine under him. What had happened?

He turned, and his shirt sleeve passed by his face. The faint whiff of explosive accelerant still on his skin brought a sharp reminder of his recent activities. The picture coalesced in his mind then, the destruction and mayhem at the Agency station, and their swift retreat to the safe house.

"Feeling better, Captain?"

Temms opened his eyes to find pretty blonde Nikki bending over him, her smile fond and warm, a familiar form indeed. A wave of disorientation washed over him. Did he remember that Nikki had been...a man? No. That couldn't be.

He pushed himself into a sitting position, swinging his legs over the side of the bed with Nikki's help. They were in a small bedroom decorated in blues, thick, slatted plastic blinds covering the windows. "What time is it?"

"Morning. You've slept through the night." She handed him a steaming cup, then stepped back, leaning against the small desk in the corner.

He sniffed at the hot liquid. It smelled like kaffe. But then so had the batch that had sacked him the night before.

C.T.'s deep chuckle came from the doorway across the room.

"It's straight up, Temms. If you want, I'll drink it first. Just to show you."

Temms took a long drink, wetting his dry throat. It was some of the best kaffe he'd ever consumed. "Pretty low trick."

"Agreed." His friend came into the room. "Wasn't my idea, actually. That would be your crew who suggested it. A man can only take so much before he breaks. And we need you whole." He held out his right hand. "Don't you feel better?"

Temms put the cup into his left hand and shook C.T.'s with the other. "In all honesty, I do. Ready for action now, though. How's the radar?"

"Nothing's come near the house all night. I think we've succeeded in a clear getaway."

"We're in debt to Pinsan and Hocai, then." The shuttle pilots had done well, hiding the flitters. He drained his cup, feeling the stims course through him. He felt a whole lot more like himself. "How long till evac?"

C.T. checked his watch. "Still have a couple hours."

Nikki smiled, a dimple appearing in her left cheek. "I could whip you up a great breakfast. Promise it'll give you all the energy you need for the day."

"Ah…sure, why not?" Feeling a little self-indulgent, Temms stretched. His stomach growled. "Apparently my belly agrees."

"Good." Nikki got to her feet and left the room.

Temms rubbed his forehead, finding his mind a little clearer than it had been of late. "Any news on the Agency front? Any retaliation?"

"Nothing. Very low profile. After the breaking news report last night, it's been nothing." C.T. shrugged. "Garrett sent a message to Nik. Everything at the station seems to be the same. Four Agency ships, all in orbit. The station's shields are up."

"Anything from the Consortium?"

"Not yet."

"Maybe they're still on the fence."

He said it with conviction, but he wasn't at all sure of that.

It burned him a little that the Agency hadn't swiftly responded to their little demonstration. But they hadn't developed into a strong, powerful influence in the sector by acting without thinking. Even if some Agents were vindictive little weasels like Delcin, the power structure contained others who thought out long-term plans and controlled outlooks.

Like Tuon Donn.

He'd expected the legendary Agency head to have come to visit the station, this new bauble he'd acquired. But monitoring the usual frequencies and what scanning he'd been able to do of the agency ships hadn't revealed his presence.

The smells of something delectable came from the kitchen, and he got to his feet. "That girl is one amazing cook," he said, heading out the door.

"You think so? You should taste the *jumma* stew that Nicholas puts together. Gourmet quality."

"Nicholas?" Temms said. His feet slowed to a stop as he reached the kitchen, where Riviera was already at the table, enjoying a plate of eggs. "Last night? You mean, that was real?"

C.T. laughed. "After all the things you've seen in both universes, you're still surprised by something? I'd say this should be one of your special days. Make a note."

He moved past Temms, taking a plate and a cup of kaffe before he sat at the table.

Temms approached the cook, automatically taking the plate Nikki held out to him. She winked.

He just shook his head. He couldn't even explain the actions of his fellow humans. How could he hope to understand the variety of aliens he'd met?

The food was delicious, and those around the table engaged in lighter conversation, setting the events of the past few days behind for now. Nikki leaned close to Temms, a faint, sweet aroma of lotion or perfume released at her movement.

"Val and I have been debating the name of your ship, Captain. Surely you could have chosen something more inspiring?"

He chuckled. "If I had chosen, perhaps I could have."

He explained the Confederation's tradition of the captain naming the new ship for his subordinate who's about to take command. "I've long had the habit of discarding ideas in discussion as doubtful, preferring other options. My captain played a gigantic joke on me by naming my ship after that unfortunate habit."

"Now that you've started over in a new universe, as Garrett has, I'd think you could rename it." She batted blue eyes at him in a flirtatious way.

"I suppose I could." He hadn't really considered it. "You know, I think the name's grown on me. It's more like a challenge, especially when I'm being underestimated. I've got to live up to a higher standard than that name. We have to crush our doubts and move on."

C.T. waved a fork at him in emphasis. "Anyone who's underestimating you," he mumbled through a mouthful of eggs, "deserves what they get."

"Thanks for that vote of confidence, my friend." He raised his mug in salute.

"To success," Nikki said, and clinked her own mug with them.

Finishing up, Temms found himself pleased with exactly where he was.

First breakfast, then back to the ship, then back to the fight.

CHAPTER 3

IN the stark room with the iridescent white walls that the Ancient had given them to use as a dormitory style bedroom, Liang Chao Chen lay on the hard cot, blankets pulled over her head. It was her rest period, but she hadn't slept for a moment.

She'd cried. She'd cursed. She'd silently castigated herself for being the biggest fool since the worlds were born. Slumber, however, had escaped her.

Part of the problem was her sore ribs and the knee that wouldn't stop aching. The pain flashed in her consciousness like a neon light, reminding her of the consequences of trusting Nim Williams with her heart.

When she'd realized they were both trapped on the Ancients' space station, with the enemy Agency boarding their occupation forces, she'd believed Nim was out defending them against the Agency incursion. Hoping to assist, she'd hurried down the long corridors after him.

Only to find him sabotaging the force fields and letting the Agents inside.

The vision of him three days before standing at the control box with tools in hand brought a wave of nausea splashing over her. His betrayal of their mission alone brought her a physical ache that had settled in to her bones after the invasion. The fact he'd physically attacked her and knocked her unconscious, after his promises of love, after she'd loved him, after she'd let someone close for the first time. This is what she'd received in return. Pain. And sorrow.

After the Agency invaded the station, Liang had passed in a haze through the confusion that followed, even once the Agency goons had brought her to the control room. She'd hit her head harder than she had thought.

No, Nim hurt me more than he should.

A sob forced itself from her chest, despite her exhaustion. Like the others that had preceded it, that cry of defeat sucked more of her will away. Her state of being confounded her. She felt much more crushed than when her parents had died, leaving her an orphan, or even when Kevan had sold her to fat Oke Runyon to pay his bills. Then she was angry—with fate, with those at fault for her downfall. She could turn that anger on those responsible and fight back, and she always had. She was a strong fighter with a strong heart.

But in this, she had betrayed herself. It was the ultimate failure.

She wiped tears from her eyes and tried to find a comfortable position on the thin mattress. There wasn't one.

"Miss Liang?" The soft whisper came from the cot by the far wall.

Disappointed in herself, Liang groaned, trying to smother most of the sound in her pillow. Silence stretched out in the room, and she eventually uncovered her head far enough that she could speak, though she didn't turn her tear-swollen face to the young alien. "Yes, Uri?"

A rustle of bedclothes came from the other cot. "Are you all right, ma'am? Can I bring you anything?"

Hating the idea that anyone found her pitiful or needy, she wiped her face and forced herself to sit to face him. The young one of the Muuvo race sat, hunched-over, on his cot, his stocky, short body solidly planted. Long sleeves covered the tiger-like stripes on his lower arms. He studied her with large, black eyes that seldom blinked.

"I need nothing," she said softly. "You are kind to offer."

He hesitated, the thick fingers of his hands laced in his lap. "Do you think the Captain is negotiating for our release?"

"The Captain has not forgotten or abandoned us, Uri. This you may be sure of." A warning seeped into her mind, and she got up, limping to a nearby counter where someone had left a stylus and paper. "We are not alone here on the station." She wrote, *The Agents are likely listening to everything we say. Installed spy devices everywhere. But don't give up hope of rescue.*

Palming the note, she returned to her cot, surreptitiously dropping the paper in his lap.

He looked up at her, his expression confused, but he read it. Then his face lit with understanding. "If you say so, Miss Liang."

She managed a faint smile. "If I'm not sleeping, I suppose I should head back to work." She didn't get up, though, reluctant to encounter Nim.

Uri squirmed a moment. "*He's* not there. The Agent sent him down to the hydroponics room."

Her jaw tightened. That was almost worse than the callous

trouncing of her heart—that everyone knew it for what it was. Nim had been segregated from them since Tommy Rogers had offered to separate his head from his neck after his betrayal became public.

Uri's comment was well-meant, though. While her tongue prepared a sharp retort, she choked it back. She shouldn't take out her frustration on him.

"Then I have no excuse at all, do I?"

She got off her bunk and crossed the room to wash her face at the small sink. The mirror over the sink reflected a pathetic-looking, pale version of herself, hair rumpled from hiding under the blankets, dark circles under her eyes. *A long time since I've looked this way. Long enough.*

Splashing cold, cold water on her cheeks , she then scrubbed them till they were warm and pink. Their team was in crisis, under threat from both the Agency and the Ancients. She couldn't let a mere man get under her skin.

Staring herself down until she believed it, she grabbed her jacket from the foot of her cot and pulled it on, already thinking ahead to her plans for the rest of the day. "Everything will work itself out, Uri. Get some rest."

"Yes, ma'am." The young one dutifully tucked himself into his bed.

Liang felt an unexpected smile reach her lips. Even though she was only eighteen, and Uri perhaps four years younger, he acknowledged her status. *At least someone still obeys me.* With that little lift to her spirits, she flipped off the lights and headed down to the control room.

No one crossed her path between their makeshift sleeping quarters and the heart of the station, which still mystified her. Despite the Agency's thirty-man security squadron on the Ancients' station, the *Doubtful* crew aboard still had quite a bit of freedom to move about. Guards were always posted outside the power plant of the station, inside the control room, and along the hallway to the docked Agency vessels. But the long, empty, white corridors echoed with only the sound of her bootsteps.

Her current task, assigned by the Ancient who still masqueraded as the jovial Captain Jak Moster, was to decode the language needed to locate the parts to activate the next level of the station's capabilities. Someone had ascertained that she'd been part of the team to decode the earlier artifacts on Captain Rogers' ship, so it was assumed she was the one to "make it happen."

Stepping in the room, she took a quick survey of the situation, finding a seething Tommy Rogers sitting on the sidelines as Benzi Quinn and Uri's brother Iov worked on a computer program. "What have I missed?" she asked Tommy.

"Nothing." He leaned back in his chair, arms crossed tight. "More days of nothing." He glared at Agent Delcin, who stood near the main panel, not looking at them, head plainly cocked in their direction, listening.

The bald, pudgy, soft-bellied Moster looked up from his seat at a console near the center of the room. "Now that the first officer is here to distribute orders, perhaps we'll make more progress."

"Perhaps we should have kept that lunatic boy here," Delcin growled, "to use as leverage. Several of them seemed to care what happened to him."

Liang felt, rather than saw, Quinn get up behind her, projecting a red-hot aura of anger. "You leave that boy out of our discussions, bastard. He's not for you to play with."

She held out a hand, palm forward, to shut off any further outbursts from Quinn. The look they exchanged verified they understood each other's position: for once they weren't each other's enemies, but instead were united against a common antagonist. *Strange to be allied at last. But it is the way of things.*

She eyed the Agent, gesturing at Moster. "Agent Delcin, as you are surely aware by now, we did not build this station, nor did we create this language. If those who crafted this complex cannot decipher its mysteries, I don't understand why you fault us for failing to do it?"

She delivered this in the mildest voice she could manage, but she couldn't cover up the steel resolve underneath. None of them intended to provide the Agency with the information they wanted, even if they could come up with it. Soon enough the Agent would be tired of the extra trouble having the *Doubtful's* crew around caused, and quit pushing them to solve the riddles of operation.

But what happened then? If they were expendable, then they were expendable.

This was why they'd agreed to make little bits of progress, as slowly as they could, preferably discovering things not related to the functions of the station. For example, Iov had brought to the Agent's attention the control he'd activated to vent noxious gases from the science lab to open space. The tube was approximately five centimeters wide, not large enough to space any of the crew, and ran about three meters from the lab to a port. Moster had nearly discorporated into the Ancient's gaseous form when that tidbit had been shared.

"No, no! This is useless. We need controls for the power conduits!"

Iov had bowed and scraped and looked in every way as though he was trying his very best to please his new masters. But the *Doubtful* hostages understood exactly how useful that information was going to be: not at all.

The Agent wasn't impressed with her response. He crossed the room to stand next to her, much closer than he should have. Head and shoulders taller than she, he waited until she looked up to meet his eyes, reinforcing the fact he towered over her. Signs of his comfortable lifestyle showed in his slightly slack jaw, his thick belt, the ample cut of his jacket. He was so close that if she had her knife, she could have disemboweled him with ease. *But they took it away. Smart on their part.*

"Miss Chen, you're a bright girl. I know you don't misunderstand me. I need results. I will *have* results."

He grabbed her forearm, digging his fingers into her skin. In her current, tender state, the action triggered an unbidden, instinctive response on her part. Her fist balled up and landed in his crotch.

Delcin groaned and stumbled backward. Two of his goons ran up to seize her, one taking each arm, forcing her to her knees. Tommy jumped to his feet. Benzi did, too. The guard by the door straight-armed Tommy across the throat, knocking him to the ground. Another powered up his weapon and aimed it at Benzi, who hung back out of reach. She caught a glimpse to the left of Iov, face set like rock, with a spanner in hand. Four solid guns against a spanner? Not much of a contest.

"Stand down," she commanded, seeing the readiness for rebellion on all the faces. "We'll prove nothing by our deaths."

"Depends how much of an arse-kicking we give them first," Benzi muttered.

Her promise to Uri echoed in her head. The Captain hadn't forgotten them. It would just be a matter of time. "We'll try our best, Agent Delcin," she said sweetly.

The Agent still leaned against the opposite console, his body half-curled protectively around his injured parts. "See that you do," he forced between his teeth. "Let her go."

The goons released her. He gestured to them to accompany him, and the three left the control room, Delcin walking like an elderly man. The remaining guards took up a position at the door, whether to keep them in or anyone else out, Liang couldn't say.

She resumed her seat, checking visually on each of her crewmates. Benzi seethed in the back. Iov's thick body stood hesitantly between Liang and the door. Tommy Rogers got up slowly, a bruise already forming on his upper cheekbone.

"Well, now, this is hardly productive," Moster said, holding his arms out wide, a so-fake smile plastered on his lips. "Please, children, where's the amusement in delaying this objective? Better to just get this over with and experience the magnitude of the station's potential, wouldn't you say?"

Tommy growled at him. "I'm all for ending this lousy game."

Liang's new-found resolution took over, and the shimmer of an idea coalesced in the back of her mind. "Ensign Rogers, can you help me with this program?"

He balked, but she eyed him till he complied. He slouched over to sit beside her. Jak studied them briefly, but his console beeped, returning his attention to the screen in front of him.

"Are you all right?" Liang murmured.

Tommy just shrugged, his eyes blazing.

She tapped on the keys in front of her, opening her work session. "I just remembered that we forgot an important piece of the translation program back on the *Doubtful*."

His brow furrowed, he focused on her. "We did?"

"We did." She searched through the obfuscatory work she'd done already, looking for one section she'd particularly skirted around. It was true they needed more actual parts to construct the apparatus that would activate the upper level functions of the station, but they'd found holes in the data as well. She chose a section and highlighted the gap.

"Why didn't we know this until—"

She put a hand over his where it lay in his lap, and squeezed it, hoping he'd get the message to shut up.

He glanced down at her hand, startled. "You're not making a play for me, right? Because this isn't the time."

She yanked her hand back. "Obviously you hit your head harder than I thought." She indicated her monitor. "The only way we can receive the data is from the ship, from *our* science banks."

His eyes widened with understanding. "Oh. Oh. Sorry. Right. Our science banks. On our ship. The ship where we want to be." He nodded. "So we should, uh, contact them."

She tried not to roll her eyes. "What a wonderful idea. Why don't we share this news with Mr. Quinn? When we're ready, I'll notify the Ancient. If he's desperate enough, he should allow the exchange. It's not much, but it's a beginning."

Still nodding, he stood, backing away from her. He stumbled, and Liang wondered if he really had a concussion. *We've all got hurts to mend. The sooner we get back to our own ship, the sooner we get help.*

She forced the thought of Nim from her mind and concentrated on the data she wanted to get. Then she got to her feet, in full work mode again, headed for Benzi Quinn's station.

CHAPTER 4

AGENT Kile Delcin dismissed his guards at the door to his newly acquired office on the station, feeling free to limp piteously to his chair and collapse.

Damn that woman. If the Ancient hadn't particularly instructed that all the *Doubtful* crew aboard were to be kept safe and sound, he would have dispatched her to his own ship for some serious rehabilitation. Preferably the electric shock chamber.

That would be the last time the little bitch is disrespectful to me.

Soothing himself with the vision of Liang Chao Chen writhing in agony as she was "retrained," he settled more comfortably into his chair, but didn't find contentment there. He missed his polished wood furniture and the other luxuries he'd traded for the standard Agency officer issue on the *Shelim*. Everything here was fashioned out of the nondescript white plastic in various thicknesses. The sameness annoyed him. He deserved better.

Sorting through the piles on his desk did nothing to pacify him, either. Only frustrations waited, curled in piles of paper and data pads, ready to cut his throat.

He'd thought himself clever to track Temms Rogers' movements, his contacts, detecting that first encounter when the space station revealed itself. Days had passed while he continued his stealthy watch, waiting for the exact moment to strike. When Rogers had deposited his crack translation team on the station and then flown away. Zero hour.

It should have gone so smoothly.

They'd entered the station with ease, thanks to their man on the inside, and in a matter of minutes had established control of the station. Anticipating that the station owners would be a problem, he'd come with a fully armed team, ready for a battle if one awaited. To his surprise, not only did the mysterious Ancient appear as the unfortunate Jak Moster, who was eminently easy to deal with, he seemed perfectly happy to conduct business directly with the Agency, instead of Rogers' people.

It should have gone smoothly.

Instead, the situation had engendered one problem after another. And the worst yet to come.

Delcin's eyes fell on the communiqué he'd received earlier in the day from the office of Tuon Donn. Not from the man himself, of course. He had *people* for that. Donn had risen to the position as head of the Agency through a combination of incredibly fortunate timing and some otherwise very dirty dealing, only hinted about in the back halls of the safe Agency compounds. That reputation alarmed those who had to face him, as it was likely meant to.

While he'd met Donn at ceremonies or other official events, he'd never had the dubious pleasure of Donn's interest in his work. Consequently, Delcin was certainly at least concerned, if not quite alarmed at Donn's terse announcement of his impending arrival.

He'd hoped Donn was coming to celebrate Delcin's capture of the space station, which was an unexpected conquest on the Agency's agenda. But he wasn't. Instead, his visit was occasioned by Temms Rogers' blatant destruction of the field office at Primor'e.

The ache in his crotch waning, Delcin opened the bottom drawer of his desk and pulled out an elegant silver-plated flask and a small etched glass. Both had been confiscated from a rebellious mercenary ship captain whose name Delcin had forgotten almost immediately. The contents, however, were considerably higher up the quality scale from what had been in it then. His hand trembling just the slightest amount, he poured exactly two-fingers-depth of the superior aged liquor into the glass and sipped it slowly, letting the slow burn of the alcohol going down his throat soothe him.

When he felt ready to begin again, Delcin tapped an info screen on his desk and watched the holographic transmission of the Primor'e attack. As it had the last time he'd watched, and the time before that, when he came to Rogers' defiant stand at the end, his blood boiled. And again, he was constrained by the Ancients' orders not to take retribution against Rogers' crew members in his custody.

The only sure thing was that Rogers wouldn't be far from the station as long as his people were there. Delcin held the bait that would keep Rogers close. No need to rush. An opportunity would arise to strike back at him.

But it should be a way that only removes the personnel from the ship. Surely what Jal Burko said was true. Some amazing technology is installed on that ship, ripe for the taking.

Donn would approve that measure. When the time came.

More important to Delcin was his immediate next move. He'd have to coerce the assistance of the *Doubtful* crew quickly, in an upwardly-spiraling pressured effort, in order to have some sort of results before Donn could arrive. If there was at least progress here, perhaps he could be forgiven the failure to contain Rogers and his co-conspirators.

As the co-conspirator issue pierced his mind, Delcin turned again to the holo, reviewing the participants in the disaster. Rogers, certainly, he recognized.

A bit of research identified the other leader as Charles Dutton, mercenary captain of the *Fuego*. A further push revealed that Dutton was the partner of known psychic Kyndra Vilsin. He scanned quickly, but didn't see the striking redhead on the premises of the headquarters building. Agency intelligence set out clear warnings regarding Kyndra. If Delcin wanted to put pressure on the group, that would not be the place to start.

So, who else did he have? A huge black woman with shoulders broader than Delcin's own, who took orders from Rogers. Several other non-descript men in black who came in with Dutton. And most interesting, an unseen force that took out his security men, then blasted through the front door to become—what? At some point in the process, a black-haired man appeared from nothing.

Rogers has a shapeshifter? A Bellonan?

Delcin had read reports of the capacities of these beasts, how they could shift form from animal to human, and then shift through a trick of light into invisibility. They were fierce guards, loyal and without the code of morals that governed most humans.

More importantly, was it a herd-bred Bellonan wrested from the tight-fisted grip of the Consortium? The Agency had attempted many times to buy mated pairs to begin their own herds and had been refused.

How had Rogers succeeded?

Delcin scanned quickly through, finding only the one. But did he have a pair? Could they breed outside of the carefully-monitored Consortium herd?

Possibilities whirled through his head. Much more at stake than whatever other-worldly tech might be aboard Temms Rogers' ship now. He'd have to find a way to get aboard and....

No, wait.

Delcin had the information source he needed already at hand: the *Doubtful*'s number two security man, Nim Williams. He was a graduate of the Sol Aeris school, which long ago had seen the benefit of a steady income stream from the powerful Agency coffers. All they had to do was allow the Agency to seed some specially chosen students with a switch that could be activated to bend them to the will of the Agency at an appropriate moment in time. The students were never told of their alteration, and no one was the wiser.

Nim Williams bore a special chip in his body that resonated only when singled out with a burst of an energy frequency reserved to use of the Agency. When the *Shelim* had docked with the Ancients' station, Delcin's people scanned the station in hopes of finding one of their sleepers. *And there he was.....*

He'd handily let them in, even betraying his own officers in the process. The little female was black and blue for several days after her defeat at Williams' hands. She seemed more than usually annoyed by this. Had there been more to the relationship? *An idea worth exploring.* But first, the shape-shifters.

Delcin hit the intercom button on his borrowed desk. "Williams, report to Agent Delcin's office immediately."

He didn't wait for a reply. Instead, he grabbed a data pad and a stylus and scribbled notes about the shifter and everything he wanted to know. Strange that Captain Rogers wouldn't have sent such a weapon to the station in the first place, if he'd had one available. Of course, they weren't much help technically. Everyone knew they didn't have many skills in the sciences. But as a security force, Bellonans were incorruptible and powerful killers.

Could they be wired with one of the chips? He didn't know. He sent a message to the *Shelim* to set some of his minions scouring Agency records to see if they'd ever captured a Bellonan and whether that had been tried. If Kile Delcin had one of those clawed monsters at his command, he imagined it wouldn't take long before Tuon Donn sat up and took notice. Or perhaps Donn would no longer be the one people sat up and took notice of. *Oh, the possibilities.*

His grin moved into place like a stowaway securing a warm corner in the back of a freight cargo box, determined to remain. He poured himself another very-careful two fingers and waited for Williams to arrive.

CHAPTER 5

THE day after they had rendezvoused with the *Doubtful*, returning from Primor'e, Temms was rousted from bed by an alarm that denoted the ship was under attack.

"Captain to the bridge!"

Kai Windthorp's strident call set Temms' blood racing. Surely this had to be the Agency response to his attack. He yanked on his clothes and took the ladder up two rungs at a time. When he stepped onto the bridge, his gaze sought the forward monitor screen for a visual explanation. He found his ship faced by three of the lighter Agency flyers, what would have been called frigates in the Confederation hierarchy. They were half the size of the *Doubtful*, which despite its name, carried plenty of punch. The trio fired off a volley of shots as they passed by the ship, causing minor joggles, but the shields held true.

"What's our status?" he asked, taking his seat. One stab of his left index finger brought up data on his personal monitor, real-time stats and damage. He scanned the columns of numbers as he awaited an answer.

Kai didn't look up from his board. "No damage sustained. Their weapons aren't strong enough to penetrate our defenses."

"Take evasive maneuvers," Temms said, contemplating his options. The large Agency cruisers had heavy guns. He'd learned in the fight with Burko that cruisers like Delcin's *Shelim* could take their toll on his craft. Why hadn't Delcin sent a bigger ship against him?

Better to count our blessings that he didn't.

"Yes, sir."

The aerial battle continued for several more minutes, with the frigates making repeated passes, like hungry pack dogs trying to take bites out of a larger predator. When it was clear they had no effect on the *Doubtful*, Temms expected them to pull away and regroup, but they kept coming.

"Hail them," he said to Tasiq, at the communications board.

"Hailing them now." Tasiq poked at his controls. "They won't respond, but we register that we're locked onto their system."

"Good enough for me."

Temms pondered a moment, then spoke. "Agency ships, this is Captain Temms Rogers of the ship *Doubtful*. Call off this attack immediately and your ships will be saved. Persist, and we will retaliate."

He watched the screen for some physical response, but they continued with their attack.

"You sure they're receiving?" he asked.

"Yes, sir."

He sighed. "Well, we'll do it their way, then. Kai, target their weapons. Engines if you must. Navigator, be prepared to drop below them and head back to Terza as soon as we're clear."

They acknowledged his orders. The familiar sound and feel of the lasers firing, targeting their enemies actually made Temms a little nostalgic for his Confederation days in battle. But he no longer commanded a warship. Now he was a mercenary. He didn't want to harm the Agency people. He just wanted his own crew intact once again.

*   *   *

WHILE Liang and the junior Rogers flirted over at her computer, Benzi Quinn grumbled about their idiocy and hunched over the keyboard at his own terminal, the one he'd brought from the *Doubtful*, as he muttered through his model. He nearly had it now, the answer they were all looking for.

But what would it cost them to get that answer, hmm? Little old Benzi Quinn plans to hold out awhile for this one.

Seemed to him that the part they were looking for had several different qualities. Did that mean it combined two different substances to create a third element? That third element didn't occur naturally anywhere in this planetary system, but if it was produced, it would jack this station up brighter than old Makayla's twinkling eyes.

That memory brought him up short, and he paused, lost in the past with the dark-eyed barmaid he'd dallied with in the months before he'd gone to space. Perpetually happy, Makayla buoyed him up in the bad days after his father died. Even now, he sometimes saw those eyes in his dreams, and the separation from her was relived in all his pain and glory.

'Cause you ran out on her without even sayin' goodbye, you lowlife. Couldn't

face it for yourself, so you gave her no closure either. Some kinda man you are.

He yanked himself out of the past with a start. Benzi had plenty of self-loathing to go around. The only warm spot in his life now was Monty.

And Monty was gone.

He's better off there, back on the Doubtful, *than he'd be here, and you know it. Bleedin' Agency's like to shoot any of us as look at us, and that's the truth. Okalani and the Cap will make sure he wants for nothing.*

Nothing except his Da.

The sense of loss of his adopted boy swept over him, and his fingers blurred in his sight, hitting some wrong keys that set off a torrent of alarms. The Agency grunts watching over them came to attention, weapons in hand, and Benzi stiffened, suddenly aware he was front and center.

"Sorry, sorry," he mumbled. "Need some rack time."

"I'll handle it," Liang said. She and Tommy came over to Benzi's station. She studied him a moment and then nodded. "Everything's all right here, isn't it?"

Benzi shrugged. "Just fantastic, ma'am. Captured by two enemies at once. Very efficient."

She eyed him. "Look, can you devise an underlying communications frequency?" She quietly explained the set-up she had envisioned. "If we're going to be allowed to call the ship, I want to be able to pass what intel we can back to them."

Now that sounded somewhat interesting. Had the Ice Princess come up with that all on her Lonesome? Benzi glanced up at Tommy, who rubbed his neck idly, a thundercloud on his brow. *He don't like depending on old Benzi Quinn. Not good enough for him. Well, I'll show him just how good I can be.*

"How do we know Fat Boy over there ain't gonna peel anything we attach right out of our message?"

Liang followed his gaze to Moster. "My analysis of his skill set indicates he's not capable." She turned back to study Benzi. "And your skill set is very capable."

Was that a compliment?

Benzi waited a moment to see if lightning shot out of the ceiling, and it really was the end of the world—why else would she be nice to him—and then tapped idly at his keyboard. "Well, yes, ma'am. I'll get right on it."

"Good. When you're ready, report to me, and I'll let the Ancient know we need to contact the ship for vital information. Mr. Rogers, you and I will formulate the message, so it's ready to send when the time comes."

Tommy nodded and moved away, taking a stroll around the entire control room before returning to sit at the console he'd been assigned.

Liang crouched down behind the terminal for just a moment, glancing at the guards. "They're losing patience. The quicker the better."

Benzi found a warmth and vulnerability in her eyes he hadn't seen before. As much as it irked him to admit it, she'd become human to him after her betrayal by that cockass Williams.

"You got it, ma'am."

She got up and returned to her workstation.

Did I just see her smile at me? What in the mothering universe?

He sensed a presence at his elbow a moment later, and spun to face the threat, fist clenched, but it was only Iov. "Don't sneak up on me, you bleeding wog."

The Muuvo stepped back, large dark eyes focused on the floor in apology. "I am sorry. I felt your worry for the small one. I, too, worry about Nev."

The gentle statement took Benzi off guard. His first reaction was panic that the wog had read his thoughts. His second was that the reminder of Monty's absence, echoed in Iov's compassionate tone, struck him hard.

"I—I can't help it. I miss the little guy. He was just startin' to open up, y'know, and now this. Bet it's set him to regress. We'll have to start all over again if—when we get back."

Iov smiled, and the gesture brought light to his whole face, like a slow-developing sunrise. "The captain and crew will do well by them both. It is a family, this crew. We have felt so welcomed by every member, especially you. We are in gratitude, always."

Iov bowed to him. Actually bowed, with an odd little hand gesture that felt subservient.

Welcomed by me? These wogs? Were they smoking something funny?

But Iov continued to consider him with those wide dark eyes, and Benzi's heart warmed with an empathy he didn't even want to know he had.

"Yeah, yeah, whatever," he said, brushing off the Muuvo's compliments. "Now look here, we got our orders." He drew Iov close to the monitor and typed in some preliminary specs for comm transmissions. "You know anything about this stuff?"

Iov nodded, replying with a low voice like Benzi's. "Before we came to your ship, I worked with the decryption unit of the freighter we rode. I have many times scanned through communications for hidden messages."

"How about the reverse, pal? Can you hide the messages?"

Benzi adjusted the tilt of his screen as one of the Agency guard strolled past. *Hope Iov's savvy enough to let him go before he answers.*

Iov fiddled with the tools in his hand until the man was out of earshot, then leaned close. "Of course." His face lit up again. "We are sending messages home?"

"We surely are, my friend. Let's get to it!"

* * *

IT took two days, but the collective brain trust of the *Doubtful* crew members prepared a message to be sent over the Ancients' standard communication system that would conceal a hidden code that Tasiq or one of the other crew could puzzle out. Iov's design activated a hook to keep playing the transmission over and over once it was opened, not allowing it to close until it had been parsed by the ship's computer and the secret message discovered. Once they were ready, Liang approached Moster with her request.

The Ancient sat at a console in the center of the control room, engaged in some deep communion with the monitor. Symbols appeared and disappeared at rapid speed without him touching the keyboard, as if he were controlling the device by brain power alone. If he could do that—The possibility she had underrated the Ancient crossed her mind.

But he still can't activate the next level. Otherwise he would have already done so. They aren't omnipotent.

She cleared her throat to get his attention.

"Captain, we are in need of assistance from our own ship. As you know, we worked for some time to decode the other artifacts that we put to our own use, and our research there is voluminous. We've run into several roadblocks here, but we would be better able to assist you if we had some further files."

Might as well get whatever information I can pry out of him. She fidgeted, scuffing a foot on the pale carpet. "If the *Doubtful* is even in range."

The Ancient, still masquerading as the genial captain, grinned at her. "Oh, yes, other than a trip a few hours away to cause some mischief for our mutual Agency friends, your captain has stayed in communication range, though he's not right outside. He continues to send demands for your return."

He got up, reaching out to pat her shoulder. "He cares a great deal for all of you."

Was that supposed to reassure her? She heard a veiled threat in the words. As in "If you disappoint us, he'll be the one to suffer." Or maybe she'd been hanging around Benzi and Tommy too long. Could paranoia be contagious?

"So, if we could contact them?" she prodded.

"I'll have to ask Agent Delcin." Moster spread his hands wide. "Since we were forced to include the Agency in the process, he's requested we refer these matters to him."

She eyed him, letting her face go to stone. "Surely a race as exalted as the one that contacted me on the ship, promising such great things for the humans of this sector, can make decisions without involving the greediest humans this side of the universal rift. A simple yes or no."

She stepped a little closer, letting her face soften, curving her lips in a half-smile, the expression of a devoted student to her teacher.

"If you are someone as all-powerful as you wished us to believe, it doesn't seem right you'd have to defer every minor decision to them." She shrugged. "Besides, if this gets you what you want, you won't exactly need them any more, true?"

The deceptive amusement on the Ancient's face faltered for just a split second, then slammed back into place.

"We must succeed," he said through clenched teeth.

"Then let us help you."

Liang kept her gaze and tone steady. She had anticipated a flat no. The fact he considered her request meant a chink existed in that firm Ancient determination, one they hadn't been able to access until this moment. Could she find out what the Ancient was after? Caution was warranted, though. She couldn't appear overeager or desperate.

Even though I want nothing more than to be home.

"You'll be able to help the peoples of this universe if you activate the station?" she asked. "That's what the Captain said."

The alien's face morphed to a jolly grin. "Your Captain is right. When I have access to the upper levels of the station's power grid, I'll be able to reach the farthest corners of this star system and beyond. I

LYNDI ALEXANDER   33

will bring peace and control to even the most troubled areas."

Its eyes were warm and brown, intent on winning her over. It was all she could do not to shudder out of reach at what she knew the alien really proposed.

Enforced control, an iron grip, one more power-hungry leader trying to make people's lives miserable.

She forced her eyes open wider, as if awed. "You can do that from here?"

"Absolutely." The alien invited her closer with a sweep of an arm, indicating the computer terminal it had been using. "From this seat I can spy on areas on any planet in this system, keep order among the residents, make sure everyone is working for the betterment of their communities. If there are those who decide they want to be selfish or commit crimes against their neighbors, I can enforce the law from this station. A quick lightning bolt from the sky and—" He brushed his hands against each other. "No more trouble."

"That's fascinating," she said. "You can go even beyond the borders of the system?"

The alien ran his hand along the top of his monitor, beaming with pride. "That's the beauty of the mechanics. As it was many millennia ago, when our race first sent seeds of civilization into the various universes, once the machine is working at full capacity, the power it generates feeds its growth. When we set the station into full operational mode, we will be able to enforce peace and productivity in an ever-expanding spiral."

"A true gift to all people," Liang said, her stomach in knots.

There's no way we can allow this to proceed to full operational status. The cultures of this system and more will be doomed. Protest will be squelched from here with the push of a button. Life as we know it will be over.

"Now, you had a request?" the Ancient asked.

She held out the datatube. "Here is the message with the list of files we require."

"I will have to review this first."

"Understood."

Half holding her breath, she waited, watching over his broad shoulder as he opened the file on his monitor, hoping the trust she'd put in Iov and Quinn was justified. The list of items they'd agreed to ask for displayed as expected. Moster read over it, grunting in agreement, then closed the file.

"That's all you want?" he asked.

"That will help us make a breakthrough," she said. "I'm certain."

A breakthrough for our cause, not yours. But you don't need to know that.

She held out her hand for return of the device.

"Very well." He tapped his keyboard and entered a security code of some kind that came up as blank spaces when he typed it. "It's sent. Hopefully your captain will provide what you've requested promptly."

"Thank you," she said. "I'll let the team know to be ready."

To her surprise, the Ancient stood to return the tube to her, then leaned forward in her direction. A real bow of respect.

"I knew once you understood the usefulness of cooperation, that this activity would go more smoothly. You will be back to your ship much faster now."

She allowed a faint smile, holding back the larger triumph that threatened to express itself. "Yes, sir." She turned and walked away before her true feelings spilled over.

For the first time since the Agency had arrived, she actually had a positive feeling about their direction. Her stomach rumbled, as if in response. As reluctant as she was to eat the food the Agency had brought aboard, it was all they had.

"I'm going down to the galley," she said to Benzi. "Shall I bring you something back?"

He snorted. "What? And deprive me of my chance to get my ass out of this seat for awhile? No, thanks. I'll stop down later."

Iov was deep in work, something he was building from artifact parts, so she didn't disturb him. Tommy Rogers, though, stood to meet her, straightening his shoulders and rolling his neck.

"I'll walk you down," he said. He pushed up his sleeves and waited for her at the door.

She knew that tone. What it said to her was, *In case Williams thinks he'll get one over on you again.*

"I'll be fine," she said quietly.

"Not a problem." He grinned at her, his expression such an echo of his father's that her heartstrings tugged. If Temms Rogers was here, he'd be dealing out small bits of hell to get them all released. Now that they'd sent him some information, perhaps it wouldn't be so long until he arrived.

"If you must."

She bent to grab the shapeless jacket she'd been wearing around the station, then slipped it on. It made her feel less desirable, which in turn justified her re-establishment of a distance between herself and many of the strangers aboard. Tommy, now, she was used to. Though she didn't want him getting any ideas. Iov and Uri were thoughtful and kind, and she enjoyed their company. Even Benzi Quinn's rough banter was more comforting than annoying, by this time, and she let it feel natural.

But she wanted to feel as unattractive as possible in case she ran into Nim. She had to stay away from him. Even if it ripped her heart into bits.

The guards searched them on the way out of the control room. It had become routine, and she hardly bothered to get irritated any more. As if they had reason to steal any of the damned artifacts. Or anything else that didn't work. Tommy gave them his usual run of half-insulting suggestions where they could put their weapons, but she didn't respond in any way. What was the point?

Once clear of the checkpoint, she and Tommy walked down the hall. He offered her his arm, and she took it, not because she felt lovey-dovey, but to be able to walk close enough to whisper into his ear, sharing details of her success.

When they entered the galley, Tommy's arm stiffened under her fingers. She glanced around to discover why, and spotted Nim sitting alone at a table at the far side of the small room. A pair of Agency heavies sat at one of the other tables, leaving half a dozen empty. Nim glanced up at the same time she did, and got to his feet. She quickly looked away.

"Do you want to go?" Tommy murmured.

"Why should I leave? I've done nothing wrong," she said. But if she was so steady against Nim's presence, why couldn't she make her feet move?

"You're right, there." He walked over to the food storage closets and grabbed four packets, then set them in the warmer. "You want fish again?"

She finally wrenched her body under her control again and walked it to a table near the closet. "It's better than some of the rest."

"Liang?" Nim's voice was strained, tight.

She wanted nothing more than to ignore him, but something in his pained tone hooked her attention like the pathos of a wounded *sakna*. Her gaze slid over to him. He stood, rigid, by his table, hands in his pockets. His face was pale, his eyes distressed. Was he sorry? Or did he just resent Tommy by her side?

"What do you want?" she said, with as much snap as she could.

He glanced at the Agency men, opened his mouth like he wanted to say something, then sat down again at his table.

"He's a traitor, Liang. Just leave him alone." Tommy brought a tray to their table where he set one packet down for her and took three for himself. "I'm a growing boy!" he protested at her raised eyebrow.

"You need extra nutrients to repair all those injuries you continue to incur," she scolded.

"Hey, I'm just standing up for the good guys. That's our duty, isn't it? To fight against repression? Not like those who'd just roll over and—"

The goons got to their feet. "Shut up, will you, punk?" one said. "Makes me want to break your jaw, just listening to you whine."

The other chuckled as they tossed their waste from their trays, and they echoed Tommy's steely glare as they left the galley.

Liang stiffened, expecting Nim to make some follow-up comment to put Tommy in his place, but none came. Her surprise brought her glance up to his level. He was staring at her, practically reaching to her through his troubled eyes.

She couldn't eat, feeling he was trying to tell her something. *Or is that just the guilt I feel for being such a fool?*

Tommy glared at Nim. "You've done all the damage to this team that you're going to. Stick to your own kind."

"They're not my kind!" Nim growled.

Tommy just wouldn't let go. "You have a funny way of showing it then. Trying to kill your first officer."

"I would never hurt her," he said, his eyes on Liang. "I...."

His features warred with each other, his mouth twisted and released as he tried to form words. She tried to read his expression, but failed. She couldn't help herself. She had to know. "It was hardly an accident, what you did. How should I perceive the attack, then?"

"Liang, I had no—"

Williams, report to Agent Delcin's office immediately.

When the announcement came across the intercom, his face froze, his body stiffened, and he stood up. Without looking at her again, he turned and walked away from his table and out the door, leaving his half-finished meal behind.

Tommy speared some fruit from the packet he had obtained, and then pursed his lips. "Now, that was strange. I'll admit it. Rude, even for him."

The jerky, controlled movements disturbed her, too. Something abnormal was at work here.

"It was almost as if he moved without his own volition." A sudden compulsion to find out more overtook her and she got up, then crossed to the door. She peeked out, seeing Nim disappearing up the hall that led to the offices where the Agency held court.

"What are you doing?" Tommy asked.

"Testing a theory."

She slipped out of the galley and followed Nim on light feet. He never turned to look at her. but she didn't know if that meant he couldn't stop to notice her, or that he just didn't care.

"Nim?"

He kept walking, his feet almost dragging along.

"Nim, answer me!"

She came within five meters of him, matching his dull pace, but before she could confront him, he took a sharp left turn into an office, closing the door behind him. The sound of heavy booted feet, several sets of them, came from the hallway past the door. Liang sprinted away before they could spot her.

His behavior didn't seem to be a matter of choice. Could the Agency have controlled him? In the galley, he hadn't seemed drugged or altered, other than his struggle for words. Yet when they'd called, he'd responded, in an almost robot-like way.

Does this mean I can forgive him?

She wasn't prepared to do that just yet, not until she knew all the facts. All the same, a small corner of her heart lit up with the fire of hope once again. Maybe what they'd had was real after all. When the team had thrown off Agency captivity, they could deal with whatever hold the Agency had on Nim. They could do it, together.

But first, they had to get themselves off this accursed station. That message should be arriving in the *Doubtful's* queue just about now. She offered up a quick prayer that Tasiq or Gretta would ferret out the message quickly, and their rescue could be that much more imminent.

Letting hope buoy her, she returned to the galley to share her observations with Tommy.

CHAPTER 6

TEMMS studied reports from the other ships in his loose alliance all morning at the large black desk in his office, trying to find some chink in Agency armor. He found nothing, until Tasiq beeped his comm, his feline R's rolling even more than usual from his excitement.

"Captain, I'm passing a transmission that Liang has just sent from the station."

That caught the captain's attention.

After the incident at Primor'e had sparked a round of Agency "wanted" notifications across the system, he'd ordered the ship away from the immediate area of the station. They retreated to establish an orbit around a moon of Terza, a small rock that hardly deserved the name of a satellite. Hiding wasn't his style. Staying alive was.

"All right, Tas. Standing by."

He set his work aside and refreshed his tea, waiting for the information. All transmissions from the station to date had been from Delcin. What had changed? Was it even a sanctioned message? Or had Liang managed to subvert the communication matrix?

Impatient, he jabbed several times at the activation button, awaiting the transfer from the bridge. The message finally appeared, a terse list of demands.

Captain Rogers: In order to complete our work helping the Ancients, we will need the following files from our previous work on the artifacts....

It went on to list about twenty files, some of which Rogers was familiar with, others he wasn't. Some of the requests were for things that seemed pretty basic. Hadn't the group already taken this information when they went to the station in the first place?

Their initial reception by the duplicitous Ancient he'd believed to be Jak Moster flashed into his mind with a red-hot blast of fury. Temms had actually believed he'd been invited to be part of a miraculous discovery and opportunity to help millions in their new universe home.

But it was just another swindle. And wherever there was a swindle, an

Agency bastard was waiting to take advantage of it.

The message didn't say much more, a simple reference that they were all being well-treated, which their captors may have required. But if they already had this information on the artifacts, why were they asking for it again?

He buzzed the communications console on the bridge.

"Tas, was this all?"

"It's what we got. But something keeps hanging up the replay on this message. It's possible there's an extra layer embedded here. I'm trying to strip it out now."

"Extra later? A secondary message from the team, you mean?"

"That's my guess. I will report when I have success."

He acknowledged the request, then sat back in his chair, reading over Liang's list again. He could hear in his head that formal phrasing in her soft voice. But nothing on the list triggered any special significance for him. He sent the list on to the sciences officer with a message to gather up and bundle the files and hold them for transmission.

Where was Tommy? Was he all right?

He'd almost lost his son to an indigenous virus before they'd come across this station. Now he'd lost him again.

The story of our lives, me and Tom. We come together, then get torn apart. Over and over again.

What was it C.T. Dutton had suggested last time they'd met? That Tommy was looking for a command of his own? It hardly seemed that the boy had outgrown his ball uniform or even his cadet's jacket from the Confederation school. How could he be mature enough for his own ship?

"Not if I have anything to say about it," he muttered. One ear trained on the comm, awaiting news from the bridge, he went back to reading the day's memos.

*　*　*

NOT until the beginning of the next shift turn did Tasiq burst through the captain's door, his fur standing on end with excitement.

"I've deciphered it—they've found a way to send data!"

Temms, already rising to his feet, held out his hand for the data stub. "Are all of them all right?"

"Seems that way."

Tasiq moved behind the desk to peer over the captain's shoulder as Temms activated the message and read it.

Captain: First, we trust this message finds you all well. On the station, we have had troubled times. Nim Williams was revealed to be an Agency sympathizer—he allowed troops onto the station. Although there may be more to that story. The rest of us are pressured night and day to solve the mystery of the missing parts. The good news is that Mr. Quinn has discovered the schematics for the parts in the records, though he has not shared this with either the Agency or the Ancients. These depictions and likely materials that the parts might be made of are included in this message, so that your staff may investigate the possibility that the devices might be on a nearby planet, or otherwise concealed where one might not expect to find them.

Temms stopped reading and let those two earth-shattering revelations sink in. He had a traitor among his people. And Quinn had solved the mystery.

Perhaps some connection between Quinn and the Ancients had been formed during their contact when the Ancients helped them defeat Burko, and that bond led him to find what all the others could not.

We continue to provide the Ancient with information that leads nowhere, disclosures of material that cannot forward its cause. But our options grow more and more limited. The patience of the Agent in charge grows shorter as well. It may be only days before they initiate stronger incentives to force more productive results.

Temms didn't need the implications of that spelled out. The Agents would have no problem torturing or even killing his crew, one at a time, hoping the rest would then fall into line and follow orders.

We have no information on weaknesses of the Agency presence. The only event of significance that has come to light is the approaching visit of Tuon Donn to the station. Apparently he believes the capture of this station is a major achievement. In my opinion, Captain, this visit will be a deadline of some sort. If we can provide you more information before then, we will. Afterward, it is debatable if all of us will be here to continue to conduct the work.

The message ended. Temms skimmed it again, then skipped to the plans that showed what they were looking for.

Depicted was a rectangular object of an indeterminate gray color, approximately the size of a small footstool. One side came to a sloped bend, while the others came to perfect ninety- degree corners. When he manipulated the diagram into a Three-D hologram, he discovered a line of markings across the top.

"You recognize that, Tas? Anything we had on the bridge when

Kit was working on the device?"

The communications officer shook his head.

"May the Great Marten and Heavens above help us, trying to find something that size in such a great area of space. Five planets. Surely it would be somewhere nearby. Terza or Perpetra."

Both were well-populated planets, so that could complicate any search. *And the Consortium owns more than half that ground and air space.*

Is that why the Prince was so reticent about his ability to help?

What do they really know?

The incessant questions wrapped themselves around the tendons inTemms' neck, pulling them tight. Best to be grateful for small blessings.

"I'm lucky to have such a resourceful team. All of you." He included Tasiq in his congratulatory grin. "Get these drawings on to D, and let's see whether we can make a best guess where we can start to look."

"Yes, sir."

"Can you copy their technique? Can we send them back a message that lets them know we got the one they sent? Perhaps some way to sneak them hints of what's going on out here?"

"I'll get Gretta on it, Captain. She's got a real gift for detection and disguise."

"Good. Keep me posted."

Tasiq agreed and left the office. Temms scrolled up to the top of the message once again . While he was glad to have the information on the Ancients' device, he was more personally stunned by Liang's disclosure that Nim Williams was working for the Agency.

He thought back to his interactions with the man, their work together. He'd taken Nim with him to C.T. Dutton's ship, when they'd conspired against the Agency, and when Tommy had been down with the virus that hit so many of his people the month before, Nim had stepped into his shoes. The man had had access to every secure document that had passed through the ship. He knew many, many things that could take Rogers and his crew down.

Incensed over the betrayal of his ship and crew, only afterward did Temms recall a much more devastating impact of this revelation. Liang Chao, who for her first year on the ship had distanced herself from the male members of the crew, protecting her heart, had at last let someone in.

Nim.

His heart beat pounded in his ears, and rigid protest stiffened his muscles. Reprehensible that Nim had turned on the captain who'd hired him and the crew mates who counted on him, but the damage he'd likely done to little Liang's heart was unforgivable. It was a father's reaction to seeing his daughter dishonored.

Bad form, Williams…bad form. You'd best be ready for what I've got for you. Right after I take down that bastard Delcin.

CHAPTER 7

TEMMS collected the files from Riviera and Tasiq, everything Liang had asked for, wanting to comply as soon as possible. He had no way of knowing how long this method of communication could be maintained, so he had to take advantage of it.

Dani personally assembled the crate of parts on the main deck of engineering.

"Too bad we can't tuck some explosives in it. Bet that would get the Agency out of the picture fast," she complained.

"Whatever we send will be scanned and scrutinized, D. Can't take the risk of raising suspicion." He stretched weary muscles. When had he last had a solid night's sleep? He couldn't remember. The edges of his thoughts were beginning to fray on a regular basis.

She poked at the crate. "I don't know how any of this will help. All these items are on the inventory from the list Benzi took with him when they went over with you."

"Maybe they won't." He took the data pad and read over the requested entries. "It could have been just a vehicle to get their other message here, and to receive a message back. Gretta put together a burst message tacked to the confirmation to let them know what we're doing to help them. Bottom line is, if we're going to keep the conversation going, we need to play along."

"Understood." She crossed her arms, studying the box. "I sure hope they get back soon. I don't know how long Monty will hold up."

The captain glanced behind them to the table where the boy sat on a tall stool, hunched over a pile of artifacts, idly stacking them. "How is he?"

"He won't let me out of sight range. He's really regressed, Captain. Now he's stopped talking altogether. All I can get out of him is an occasional whimper." She chewed her lip, then looked Temms in the eye. "He needs his dad."

Feeling that guilty burden settle onto his shoulders like a lead cape, Temms nodded. "We're doing everything we can, D. The shield keeps us from getting too close. Short of a suicide mission to storm the station, we don't have many options. But finding whatever it is they're looking for may be the key. Any leads on the device?"

"Nothing yet." She led him over to Benzi's office, where a temporary work station had been set up for several of the science officers. Temms noticed Monty's anxious gaze following them in. *Poor kid. We've got to get this resolved soon.*

Inside, Shiro Vered and Zandra Cilka flashed through screens of data, the specs of the requested device on the desks beside them. Both glanced up as the pair entered. "Captain," they said, almost in synch.

"How's it coming?" he asked.

"Nothing yet," Shiro replied, pausing for a drink of kaffe. She took off her rumpled jacket and rubbed her eyes. "We've moved through the artifacts originally on the ship, and they don't match. We're hoping the inventory of what has been acquired since will be more productive."

Blonde Zandra looked up at him, bangs falling in her face. "They're all right over there, though, aren't they, Captain? You don't have any reports that they're being hurt? Because—" Her face twisted in pain. Then she got control of her emotions. "It's just that Benzi...."

The small admission was another revelation for the captain. Had the rough-edged Quinn won the heart of this woman?

"The fact they got this message through proves they're all right. Every bit helps. Keep at the data, Zandra. That's what we can do for now."

"Yes, sir," she said, a hint of tears choking her voice.

Her emotion tugged at his conscience. "We'll get them all back," he said, more definitively. "As soon as we can."

She nodded, with a faint smile, and went back to her screen.

Temms turned away, caught another look at Monty, and his determination grabbed hold. His shoulders seemed to push back, and he stood taller. No time to waste. "Let's get this shipment off to them. We won't get another peek into their situation until they can reply."

"Yes, sir," Dani said.

Debating what he could send to help them along, an idea occurred to him. "Maybe we can send a little more than they expected. Send this to the cargo bay, but hold until I get there." He gave Dani a pat on the arm and headed back to his office. Once there, he summoned Tabio.

When the shapeshifter arrived in his human form, the captain gave him a quick update of the situation.

"We'll drop off the crate and data chips at the airlock to the station. I'd like you to go along. Unseen, of course."

"Of course." His lips curved in a faint smile. "Do I have orders to end these Agency monsters?"

"The team said they've easily got forty officers on the station, Tab, and reinforcements on their ship are still in range. Too many for one to handle. Even you. My orders to you are to protect our people. If they come under threat, and I imagine they will, you can take whatever action is necessary to ensure their safety."

"I understand, Captain. I am prepared to do so."

"Good. We've arranged to rendezvous with the station at the beginning of eveturn. Be at the cargo bay lock."

"Yes, sir." Tabio stood, his muscles firm as granite. "I'll be there."

* * *

WHEN the airlock opened, both sides stood, fully armed, eyeing the other. The Ancient in Jak Moster form awaited them, as well as Agent Delcin.

Delcin surveyed the *Doubtful* crew's weapons with displeasure. "We agreed on truce status, Captain."

"Yes, we did. I see that didn't keep your men from bringing their firepower."

Delcin shrugged and grinned. "Your reputation, Captain. We needed to make sure."

Temms ignored the appeal to his ego. "I want to know that my people are being treated well."

"I expected you would." Delcin gestured to one of the men behind him and suddenly Nim Williams was shoved into prominent view.

"Captain," he said, with a little nod. He stood straight, looking ahead. He didn't hold his captain's gaze.

Temms squelched his first angry response, since he wasn't supposed to know about his security officer's betrayal. He also remembered Liang's cryptic reference that there might be more to that story. "Report on the team."

"No one has been harmed, sir. Everyone is cooperating as expected."

Temms walked to the side. Nim's attention did not follow him. "Are you working with your first officer to make sure the decryption continues?"

"I—" His frozen stare flickered for a moment, then returned. "Of course, sir. The team must work together."

"How is Liang?"

"She is well, Captain."

Temms studied Nim's demeanor, unable to decode what seemed off about him. "Very well."

Jak stepped smoothly in front of Nim then, a wide smile on his fat face. "You see, Temms, everything is fine, awaiting your equipment. Please send it across."

"Yes, I think we've spent long enough," Delcin said. He snapped his fingers, and two of his men stepped forward. The others formed a line, shoulder to shoulder, blocking entrance to the station. "The equipment. Now."

Temms realized that Delcin must have anticipated him. Tabio might pass unseen when he became invisible, but it was a trick of light. His body was as substantial as ever. He couldn't get through the line of men undetected.

I'll have to think of another way to get an advantage. Maybe at the next update.

"All right. Riviera?" he said, turning his back to the Agency group. "Cancel orders, Tabio," he whispered, as his science officer noisily trundled the heavy crate across the intervening space. Unable to sense whether his shape-shifter remained present, but guessing he did, Temms turned around to watch the exchange.

The Agency men opened the crate, searching its contents for weapons or other dangerous items. Apparently satisfied, they closed it back up again and nodded to Delcin.

Jak practically capered with excitement. "I sincerely hope this will provide the breakthrough, Captain. Thank you for your cooperation."

"I certainly hope our cooperation would be rewarded with similar gestures. Perhaps you would release one of my crew."

"I'm afraid that's not possible. They've hardly been able to achieve anything, even as many as we have. I think we'll need all of them to continue."

Those on the station retreated inside their lock, and it whooshed closed.

Temms drew a long, frustrated breath, and ordered his people to do the same, then gave the order to disengage from the lock, withdrawing to a safe distance.

Let's pray this gives the team enough to win a little confidence. In the meantime, we'd best get to finding this device. Then we'll have some real bargaining power.

CHAPTER 8

LIANG eyed the stack of equipment on the cart beside her with weary trepidation. Most were duplicates of what they already had, and would be completely useless. The data files would be more interesting, especially if the captain had been able to code a message to send back an update of what was happening outside the station.

As anxious as she was to find such a note, she had to wait. Moster's attention was fixed on her now, his beady dark eyes flashing with impatience.

"So? Your captain has sent all you asked for, has he not? How soon will we have results?"

She carefully forced her face into a pleasant expression.

"Hopefully very soon. I'll spread the new data among my staff for more efficient processing." She picked up a handful of data pads. "I'll let you know when we come across something."

Moster hesitated next to her work station. "How can I help?"

Remembering he'd been instrumental in making the exchange happen, she smiled to encourage him.

"You've already done so much. Thank you for sending our request. I'm sure this will be a fruitful study."

The Ancient seemed put off by her reply, but nodded. "If you need something more, please ask me."

"Of course."

Before she could get tied into more specifics with him, Liang turned and walked away to distribute the equipment. Tommy sat at his usual post, plinking through files he'd scanned at least ten times, trying to look busy. She handed him a data pad, one she knew was a review of the artifacts already on Rogers' ship.

"Try the files on level three," she suggested, loud enough for Moster to hear.

Tommy's eyebrow raised slightly.

Her back to Moster, she shrugged and mouthed, *Nothing new, but perhaps we've missed something.*

He groaned, then covered his slip with a brisk roll of his

shoulders and a stretch.

"We need to have some exercise periods if we're to work at our most productive levels," he said. "Most of us aren't made to be clerical researchers." He shot a hostile look at Moster.

"Do what you must," the Ancient said. "Whatever will bring the fastest results."

"Good," Tommy said. "I'll get on setting that up."

Liang noted the excitement in his eyes and wondered what direction that would send the unpredictable son of her captain. His restlessness had erupted in trouble more than once since they'd arrived. Even though he was older than Liang by a couple of years, he still lacked maturity. He'd grown since he'd come aboard the *Doubtful*, of course.

We all have.

She moved on to Iov, who worked with Uri in a side room off the control area. Handing him three of the pads, she attempted to say more with her eyes than her mouth, aware that this area was likely monitored as well.

"If you come across any answers, please notify me immediately."

"Of course, officer Chen," the senior Muuvo replied.

She left them at work and moved on to Benzi Quinn, who continued to pore over schematics and other plans he'd dug out of the station's records. "Anything?" she asked.

He took the other pads from her. "I give it about a couple of shift turns before they'll expect us to come up with something new."

"Agreed."

She glanced up casually and found Moster studying them. Her reply had to be couched in her best cryptic style.

"I'm sure the new data will be enlightening," she said. "First we should do a preliminary scan for answers to our ongoing questions."

Quinn grunted. "No doubt."

He scribbled on some paper in front of him where Moster couldn't see. *Time to reveal the missing part?*

She tossed the idea around in her head. Certainly they'd given the captain and the *Doubtful* team a head start on the process. Perhaps they'd even decoded or located the device by now. It seemed the right choice.

"Get to work on that, then. Let me know what progress you make."

Quinn looked up at her with an exchange of conspiratorial eye contact. "You bet I will, ma'am."

She shared a tight smile, then returned to her own station. Picking up a matter projector she plugged it in to the computer and prepared to run the same tired scan she'd done many times before.

I should display more enthusiasm, I know. We've made some small successes. If only there's good news from the captain, then it will be easier to go on.

She stole a peek at Moster, who stood conferring now with the Agency guards watching them. Tension filled the room like an invisible, damp fog, penetrating even her bones. From what she'd been able to gather, the Agency commander was due to arrive at the station within the next several days. Some sort of major find on their part would go a long way toward keeping them all alive.

She skimmed through the index of the file she'd accessed, hoping she looked interested. She would let Quinn announce his find later that day, or perhaps the next morning. However much time they could buy—safely. Now it was imperative that she protect the well-being of those under her command. The remaining security officer she had was just as likely to explode and provoke a life-ending issue as he was to save them. The engineers were tough, but unlikely to defeat the horde of Agency thugs who'd come on the station.

But they had another security man....

Nim.

Every rib ached with the memory of his betrayal, but the frozen stare and odd gait he'd displayed when he'd suddenly left the galley the other day still haunted her. His actions held more than met the eye. She hadn't seen him again after that unexpected encounter. Was the Agency keeping him apart from the rest for his own safety, or were they afraid that contact might shake whatever hold they had on him?

Could she win him back to their side?

As she typed commands into the keyboard, she let one part of her consciousness consider what she knew about mind control.

She'd earlier believed it possible that the Agent held something over Nim's head, like a threat to a family member, or even to his crewmates. Perhaps even herself, if the Agency had known what their relationship was.

But since their arrival, no one had mentioned any implication of a liaison between the two, or tried to use that in any other way. And the Agency was slimy enough, they'd have made it clear if they'd intended to use it. Certainly she'd expect they would have brought the two of them face to face more often to make the idea firm in Nim's head that continued cooperation was necessary.

It could be something as simple as hypnosis.

Everything I know of Nim says he's too strong to let that happen. He wouldn't fall for any attempt to sway his purpose.

Painful as it was, she thought back to those moments when they'd fought for control of the entryway. He hadn't held back. His eyes had shown no recognition of how he felt about her. Whatever had hold of him was stronger than his will.

And he had a very strong will.

Flashbacks of their happier times together tormented her as she reviewed the files, needing to remain engaged in her work. He'd given her such joy, the daily buzz of excitement in her first love. If he was redeemable, if she could have him by her side again she'd do anything.

Emotion didn't serve her now. She needed to get back to logic.

It could be drugs. That would explain why they kept him apart, so they could administer whatever doses they required to keep him under their control.

But I can't imagine he'd cooperate with such a thing. He'd fight them. I know he would.

What else did that leave? Something more sinister than drugs. Something he had no chance to resist. Something...internal? A control chip of some sort, wired into his brain? Whatever it was, it had to be placed before the team had arrived at the station, because they'd had no contact before he'd opened the doors to the Agents.

And if that was true, the question became, how long had it been there?

A sick feeling came over her as she wondered how much damage Nim could have already caused to Captain Temms Rogers and the ship *Doubtful* without them even knowing he was a ticking time bomb?

CHAPTER 9

GRETTA Flan caught his attention from his right. "Captain, incoming message from Consortium headquarters. It's marked urgent."

"Let's see it."

Temms couldn't imagine what the Consortium would have to say to him at this juncture, especially in light of the last conversation he'd had with Prince Arlen when seeking help with the Ancients' station. *This should be entertaining.*

To his surprise, it actually was—as in, designed for entertainment. A trumpet fanfare opened the holo clip, followed by a burst of dramatic music. The scene was a large space in the lobby of the central building where Rogers and his team had first met Consortium representatives, a room now filled with people in expensive formalwear. A tall, white-haired man in an impeccable black jacket with silver epaulettes stood behind a polished wood podium, read from a hand-drafted scroll.

"The time we have waited for these many years has come at last. Our own leader-to-be, the Lumina, will take her place in the seat of power at a coronation to be held thirty rotations from this date. You are invited to attend the ceremony."

Temms was caught off guard by the subject of the announcement, and then by its contents. It was only further wonder when the speaker turned to look straight into Temms's screen. A voice came to him then, not necessarily in synch with the man's lips.

You, Captain Temms Rogers, have been personally invited by the Lumina to attend, with those who accompanied her when you came to meet her on our plane, for her voyage aboard your ship. A hesitation. *All of those who accompanied her. And the lost boy from Olesia. Please use the Diamond landing field, and be present no later than the hour of mid-day.*

The announcement went on in the general mode, inviting those in attendance to remain after the ceremony itself for a state dinner and other entertainments. Then it was done.

Temms thought over the invitation, wishing like hells that Liang was there to translate. Not that the words themselves hadn't been clear, but the implications of them struck him as impossible. Halian, of course, was dead. Liang, Tommy and Nim still trapped aboard the Ancients' station. Tasiq and himself were the only representatives available.

But Monty's invitation was indeed a curiosity. How did she even know about Monty?

The most telling part of the invitation was the suggestion that Aronka and Tabio were included. Certainly they had been a big part of her transport aboard the *Doubtful*. Was this one of the Lumina's first exercises of power? An effort to thwart her grandfather's vindictive ban on the Bellonans' returning to Consortium land?

If the kid's starting already, these old men are in trouble.

Riviera, who had taken over Liang's seat while she was missing, swiveled her chair to face the captain's. "Now how they think we gonna do that? Can't be a secret to no one at that level that our folk are still 'guests' of the station."

"That's a good question. Wish I had an answer." He turned to Gretta. "Are we expecting another transmission from the team?"

"We'll check later tonight, at shift turn."

"Well, we'll see what happens then." Temms forced a smile. "Perhaps they will send some sort of notice that they believe the standoff at the station will conclude by then, and that Tommy and the rest will be free to join them."

"That so?" Riviera's wide brow furrowed. "That be good news for sure, if it be true."

"Yes, it would." Temms pushed himself out of his chair. "I'm going to go break the news to Tabio and Aronka. I'm sure they'll want to go." He looked around the bridge. "Which might mean they'll be needing a babysitter. If anyone cares to volunteer."

The bridge was ominously silent.

Apparently the thought of spending a day with two small, rambunctious lizard young was more than anyone was prepared to handle at the moment.

"I'll leave that an open offer. We've got a week. In the meantime, get me everything you can on this ceremony. If there's any way we can set it to our advantage, we've got to take it. We need a break. Anything."

He grinned, and headed to the back hall, sliding down the ladder to the lowest deck. Since the new child, Chandi, had been born two seven-days before, he hadn't seen Aronka at all. Tabio had assured him his mate was fine. He took the promise at face value.

When he rounded the final corner nearest to the Bellonans' quarters, he actually stumbled and gagged at the smell, a musty, heavy odor not unlike that of a well-ripened compost pile. He leaned against the wall a moment, breathing through his mouth, still able to taste the disgusting thickness of the air. Hadn't anyone else been down here? Had Okalani certified this air as fit to circulate through the ship's systems?

We've got to land this ship soon and air this deck out.

The door to the Bellonans' quarters opened. Tabio's lizard visage peered out, then pulled up in surprise as he faded into his human countenance. "Captain? Is there an emergency?" He exited the room, coming into the hall to stand before Temms.

The captain coughed and tried to clear his throat. *Next time I'm definitely sending for them to come upstairs.* "No, everything's fine. The child is well?"

"Yes, sir. " Tabio sniffed. "You are alarmed about something. News from the station?"

"No. Something different."

He hesitated, wondering if he should speak to both of them at once. "Is Aronka available, too? I have something important to tell you."

"Of course." Tabio turned and led the way inside the rooms they'd appropriated. Temms expected the smell to be even stronger inside, but it didn't register that way. *Perhaps my olfactory cells have already died from it.*

The room was cluttered, objects that might have been toys scattered from one side to the other. The ports were covered, creating long shadows in the room. Aronka lay on a large oval mattress to the left of the living space, both Rey and Chandi curled up against her curves. Her golden eyes studied the captain with surprise and a little suspicion.

"What brings you here, Captain?" she asked, shifting into human form, beginning to disentangle herself from the younglings.

He held out a hand. "No, don't get up. I just received a rather odd announcement from the Consortium, and I wanted to come tell you personally."

"The Consortium?" she murmured, with a quick glance at her mate.

Temms gave them the substance of the announcement, including the cryptic reference to those companions of the Lumina on that earlier trip.

"That sounds to me like they expect you to attend."

Both of them brightened, the lighter tone of Tabio's scales showing the heightened excitement and adrenaline. "We may return?"

"It's not to the prince's palace—"

"No, but there will be others of our kind there. We will be able to commune with them, to share our news. Perhaps even to link up with potential mates for our offspring."

"Mates? You mean, you'd arrange to leave your children there to grow up with the others?"

Aronka's excitement faded. "No. I mean—" Her hesitation lingered like the pheromones on the air.

Temms raised an eyebrow. "You'd add more of them to our crew?"

Tabio was quick with his denial. "No, Captain. Certainly not, not without asking you. And we would not feel right seducing others away from the collective."

Aronka twisted up, until she was a little more upright. "We haven't thought through the possibilities, captain. But simply to be allowed the chance—" She brightened again. "We must show our gratitude to the Lumina."

"Of course."

"But the others?" Tabio asked, with a dusky, more thoughtful set to his features. "Some cannot go."

Temms nodded. "I'm working on that. I need to get back to the bridge. I just wanted to let you know."

Aronka inclined her head with respect. "Thank you, Captain. Your effort is appreciated. We shall look forward to this unexpected opportunity."

Temms took another look around the quarters. "Do you need anything? For the baby, I mean?"

Both of the Bellonans assured him they had all they needed. He excused himself and left the room, climbing quickly to the next deck up to breathe the fresher air. He could understand their exhilaration, a chance to see others of their kind once again.

He'd feel the same, once he and his crew were reunited as well.

CHAPTER 10

CONCERNED about the Lumina's invitation, Temms stopped into the infirmary to see if Okalani had any insight on what might make it possible for him to take the disturbed child along with him. When he walked in, he found the doctor at her desk, sipping from a tall mug.

"Do you have a minute?" he asked.

"Are you ill?" She studied him, her expression unwelcoming.

"No. I've got a question for you about the boy." He gave her a quick version of the message they'd received.

"What do they want Monty for?" Okalani set down her cup and glared at Temms. "That boy's been through enough. The longer Benzi's gone, the more he decompensates. Why would we drag him to the planet for some stiff ceremony?"

Temms shrugged, lifting his hands in a gesture of helplessness. He'd had much the same reaction. "I don't make the rules. I didn't even know the Consortium was aware of his existence."

"Well, doesn't that make you all the more worried?"

Her righteous indignation grated on his conscience. "Come on, 'Lani. How much more worried do you think I can be at this point? My people are being held hostage, the Agency is stalking us, the Ancients are demanding that we produce some unknown piece of equipment, and now we pretty much have to go play nice with the Consortium, because they're our last friends in the flipping universe!"

He hadn't meant to fight with her. He really hadn't. But ever since he'd come right out and told her he couldn't maintain their relationship, she'd been touchy.

Not that I blame her.

Blame wasn't the issue. He'd been honest. That's all he could manage right now. They still had to work together.

"So my question is, what can we do for Monty to make him comfortable for the day?"

Her eyes were cold, without sympathy. "Would you like me to drug him up? That might work."

His face flushed hot. A quick beat tapping in his temple warned him he was becoming too agitated. He closed his eyes, then counted to ten and reopened them. He was the Captain. That should still count for something.

"I want your professional opinion, *Doctor*, on what we can do to ease him through whatever requirements there are. I want to keep his stress to a minimum. If you don't have any suggestions for me, then I'll ask Dani. She's in charge of him until Quinn returns."

Her mouth made a little "O."

"I—Right. If I think of anything, I'll send you a memo."

"Thank you." He turned and left the infirmary before any more conversation could take place, and started on a circuitous walk around the upper deck. What he needed was a good, strong combat workout in the room Liang had made into a gym. But his usual sparring partners, all of them, were either captured or dead. Walking would have to do.

And the mental picture of what he'd like to do to Delcin and Moster both, when he got his hands on them again.

After he'd made the rounds, he headed back down the ladder to engineering, where Dani and her team pored over the data Tas had pried from Quinn's transmission. "Any luck yet?" he asked.

"Nothing major. From the color of the mock-up, it looks like it's not part of the artifacts we've been collecting."

She walked him up to her loft and showed him the amorphous gray of the parts in the diagrams, then gestured at the table of hunks of artifacts, most of which were a coppery red.

"Worse than that," she went on, "it looks like the actual activation mechanism has at least three sections. If we're lucky, we'll find it whole."

A familiar stress chord tingled the nerves in the back of his neck. "And if our luck keeps running the way it's been lately, it'll be in sections scattered across the universe."

"Or universes."

Universes, plural? "What—"

She sat on the corner of her desk, gesturing to the side chair for him to have a seat. "One of the key ingredients to this recipe is the why. Why would the part that activates a crucial function be missing?

"If it were simply broken or taken for repair, we'd guess that the Ancients would have another handy, just like our engine parts. Take one out, swap one in, you know? But that's not what happened, if we're to judge by the Ancients' reaction to this situation. So what else could it be?"

He'd been considering the same question, and hadn't come up with a great answer. "Stolen?"

"Perhaps. But my working theory is this: the part was removed from the station on purpose to keep the Ancients from boosting it to the next level. If we add to that the fact we know the Ancients had access to multiple universes, then it's possible the parts for this are scattered in the same way the artifacts were."

Ignoring for the moment the concept that his search just became layers more difficult, Temms rubbed his forehead idly, hoping it would stimulate his brain. "Which begs the question, who would remove it?"

Dani's gaze fixed on those moving around the first level of the deck. "I'm not sure how we'd know, unless there was a way to determine who had access to it in the beginning. Or when the beginning even was."

"You'd think if the Ancients originally had it, they would simply have activated it."

"So someone took it before that could happen."

"Someone who had access. Which presupposes it was one of the Ancients."

Dani's head snapped to look at him. "One of their own? That's odd."

"Not so odd." Temms stood up, then started pacing. "Based on what we're seeing of the Ancients now, I'd say someone got an idea that what they were up to was no good. So this 'powering up' would have been something harmful, not helpful, to the people of this sector."

The realization burned him. The Ancient that appealed to him in his dreams had seemed so genuine, so warm, asking for Temms' assistance in this great experiment that would light the way for all his fellow humans. *But even the Ancients split on the issue. Enough that one of them or more would sabotage the rest.*

"Do you think they enlisted the help of one of the local cultures?" Dani asked. "Maybe the part is hidden on one of these worlds." She grabbed up the data pad again. "Benzi's got a list of potential elements that are in the thing. We can scan for them planetside."

"On all the planets of the system? How long will that take?"

"Well, it'll take awhile." Her lips pursed as though she didn't want to say more.

Maybe some of his connections would have a better response or idea where to look. The task had definitely moved beyond a one-ship job, for sure. "We can draft some help, I'm sure. All the same, trying to find several box-sized chunks of metal across five planets…."

Even saying the words made the task feel daunting.

"Don't forget the universes."

He groaned. "How could I forget that?"

Her perky grin appeared, the one she'd nearly lost when she had the virus weeks before. If she'd died, he would have been so lost.

"We can do a search through the catalog of artifacts Kitana had before the crossover. See if there's anything that might fit the bill."

A shred of information fluttered in Temms' mind, just out of reach. Something relevant to the alternate universes discussion.

"If the rebellious Ancients were able to get artifacts into our universe, couldn't we assume we weren't the only ones?"

She cocked her head, her gaze now fixed on the ceiling. "I guess that's possible."

"So if the artifacts were seeded, to bring us here—"

"Like bait?" she gasped.

His theory took more solid form as he allowed the planks of supposition to fall in place. "Then it's possible they were not magnanimously reaching out to new species at all, but were in fact trying to get someone to bring back what was missing."

She frowned. "As far as the records show, the Confederation's stock was the only store of the artifacts in our knowledge. Where else could they have been sent?"

The nugget Temms had been racking his brain for slammed into place. "I know someone else who came here from another universe. Let's see what old Garrett Rawls has kicking around his ship."

CHAPTER 11

TEMMS laid the printed schematics on the conference table in front of him. "This is what Quinn's been able to put together from the records on the station. This *odahmeen* is the part that will activate the station's higher functions."

The meeting was taking place in the same conference room where Temms had met with Delcin, what seemed so long ago now, but not more than three months in real time. They'd been at this for the better part of a shiftturn, first taking stock of where the Alliance stood against the Agency, and then moving on to the more specific details of the Ancient's missing part.

Present were his science officer Shiro Vered, C.T. Dutton, Garrett Rawls and Nikki and the twins, Lin Hocai and Xi Pinsan.

Temms displayed the "complete' version of the *odahmeen,* the one where it was assembled, to the best of Benzi Quinn's ability to guess.

"But it's possible that when whoever hid it did so, that they disassembled the device. Our engineers on that side have determined this is the most likely way it would break apart."

He displayed holograms of the three pieces, as they broke along the planes of the device. One piece consisted of the top of the device, about fifteen centimeters deep, and half a meter across. The underparts separated into a cube, twelve cm on all sides, and a thinner, longer part from the left underside. All were gray, none of the shiny copper-colored parts they'd found earlier. Just a simple, work-serving, efficient device.

That was missing and holding my crew hostage.

As the others studied the holos, Temms forced a deep breath, willing his blood pressure not to rise.

Shiro waited with a folder of handouts, more detailed schematics, and when Temms nodded, she distributed them. The other captains studied the drawings, passing them around, turning them sideways and upside down.

Dutton finally set the last one down and shook his head. "I can't recall that I've seen anything like that. Anywhere."

The twins concurred. "We know every bit of metal on our ships, Captain, and if we'd had this, it would register. So sorry," Hocai said.

Temms' hopes flattened like a fluffy cushion under the bulk of the fake Jak Moster. "It was a long shot. I just thought that if I were getting rid of something, I'd want it to be as unrecognizable as possible."

He shrugged and took a long drink of his now-cold *kaffe*.

"Makes sense," Dutton said, with a glance in the direction of Garrett and Nikki, who were engaged in a war of whispers at the other end of the table. Eventually, the intense exchange caught everyone's attention, and everyone stared at them until they stopped and looked up, caught by the silence.

"Something you'd like to share?" Temms asked.

"It is *so*," Nikki snapped. She grabbed her comm and tapped on its face.

Garrett, relaxing back into his chair, pulled it upright, and shrugged at Temms. "Nik thinks she's seen this cube before. On my ship."

Nikki got up from the table and walked into the corner, turning her back as a hubbub broke out.

"Perhaps your theory was right, Captain," Shiro said, leaning close so he could hear her. "The parts were spread across universes so they could not be reassembled."

Temms watched Nikki as she had an agitated but quiet conversation. "So why don't we have the one from our universe?"

"Perhaps we have not searched thoroughly enough. Someone may have incorporated the piece after you first arrived, when you were short of parts. We should do another scan, particularly if we can get our hands on another part and pick up the exact chemical makeup."

He cocked his head and looked at her. "Good idea. Let's—"

Nikki gave a triumphant squeal and hurried back to the table, holding out her comm. The picture on it matched the diagram almost exactly. She elbowed Garrett. "I told you so!"

Garrett scratched his head. "Where is that?" He turned his head sideways, then the picture sideways as well.

"In Val's room. Under her bed. It's holding up the back corner where the bunk broke."

Garrett smacked himself in the forehead. "Oh, that."

"'Oh, that'?" Hocai asked, now intent on the picture. "Would you care to explain?"

"I remember it now. Got hired to fly a shipment back before I left Earth, flew it into Nocal, just outside San Fran." He rubbed his head as if it would stimulate his memory. "Guy I was supposed to deliver it to warn't there. Woman who met me only had half the money. So I gave her half the shipment."

He chuckled, a wry expression on his face.

"I mean, what was I to do? I was out the fuel and the delivery price besides. And she didn't have a real good explanation where the fella was what was supposed to pick it up. Could have been dead, for all I know. As I recall, she was none too happy, and left a couple good-sized laser burns on the *Shooter*'s tail feathers when I took off."

Nikki nodded. "When Valeni and I joined the crew, we furnished our quarters with whatever we could find. This fit exactly under the frame of the busted bunk."

Shiro chewed her lip. "Perhaps it is just as well you were unaware it could hold enough power to explode if it were jarred or otherwise damaged."

Garrett and Nikki exchanged glances, both turning a little red before Nikki dismissed the picture from her comm.

"Valeni said she'd get this over here immediately."

"Good." A little shocked at his sudden success. "When it gets here," he whispered to Shiro, "get that scan done and send it to every department on the ship. I want to know once and for all if we've got it here."

"Yes, sir," Shiro said, and hurried out.

Feeling a little better, Temms took a seat at the head of the table. "So if Garrett's got one of the parts and we have one here, do you think it's possible one's floating around on one of the nearby planets?"

Hocai laid a hand on his arm. "Based on what we've heard, it's possible. But it's also possible that the part has been sent to yet a third universe."

His jaw set. *Yeah, I know. But I didn't want to hear it.* "Who do we know who comes from a third universe? Anyone?"

No one did.

"Under those circumstances, I propose we try to find it here then. Once we have the exact alloy, as Nikki said, we should be able to trace it much more easily. We can spread out and cover as much territory as possible before...."

He trailed off, sure there would be an official deadline. So far they'd been able to fudge their timetable, asking for parts and data back and forth. But Delcin's patience would run out.

"We'll all do what we can," Hocai said. "We can pass it to the others, too. But, Captain, I'm sure you understand the size of the area we'll be searching. The chances of finding it are similar to being able to track one single rivet in this ship with a magnifying glass."

Temms nodded slowly. "That may be so. But that's all the chance we have at the moment. So we're going to do the best we can."

* * *

HE sent the others on their way, promising to share a copy of the report on the composition of the artifact once Dani had it. Leaving Shiro with orders to summon him once the piece arrived, he returned to his office to find a memo from Gretta about the Lumina's ascension ceremony. Most of it sounded like standard pageantry, speeches and celebrity endorsements, but she highlighted a series of details that seemed much more useful.

On a day twenty rotations before the ceremony, the new leader will hold audiences with selected guests, and she has the power to grant them certain concessions. Appointments are difficult to obtain, and it is best to make them early.

The thought intrigued Temms, especially in light of the invitation he'd received. Had the Lumina taken special interest in his crew? He couldn't imagine she'd asked his colleagues to send a whole team. Perhaps he stood a chance of getting one of these special audiences. Then he could secure the right to search even on Consortium land for this wretched artifact.

He fired back a memo to Gretta to secure one of the slots at all costs.

First, one of the parts appears, then we have a half-open door to our next solution. Maybe our luck is finally turning around.

* * *

VALENI and her find arrived at the ship within the hour, and Temms went to engineering to take a look at what might be one-third of the *odahmeen* they sought.

The curved piece of gray metal was roughly forearm-length, with a flat top and bottom and strange markings on one side. It wasn't particularly impressive-looking for something that would turn the invisible station into a power-wielding behemoth.

Standing beside him as he studied the thing, Valeni grinned.

"Apparently I'm lucky I didn't blow myself up, right?"

"Apparently." He walked around the table the piece sat on. "D, any chance we've got something that will mesh with it in our artifact collection?"

Dani removed the magnification goggles she wore, propping them on top of her dark hair. "Nothing comes immediately to mind. But remembering the last construction that worked, the obvious connection wasn't the one that succeeded."

Temms's mind flashed him back to that burst of light and the voice that had come to him from the Ancients' creation, when they'd been saved from Burko a second time. *The same voice that the Ancient had used to trick him into working with Jak Moster on the damned space station.* A rush of frustration jerked his hands into fists.

"We may not have Quinn, but Monty's still here. See if he's interested in helping. He seems to have an affinity for these things."

"Yes, sir." Dani made notes on her data pad.

Valeni walked around the table to join the captain, her spicy perfume drifting up to tickle his nose. The beads on her long fringed vest clicked together as she moved.

"What's this supposed to do again? Not just complete the station, but its actual purpose?"

"They haven't exactly been forthcoming with the details," he said, crossing his arms. "I'm pretty sure it's not the well-meant gift to the peoples of this universe they said it was when they first came to us."

"Seems a fair guess." She looked up, studying his face. "So why would you give it to them?"

"My people," he replied. "They have my people."

She nodded, still watching him. Her brown eyes were dark as chocolates, no flecks of hazel or green to distinguish them. "How many? Five? I don't mean to be thoughtless, Captain, but you seem like a man who appreciates honesty. Let's say this Ancient can activate the station and it becomes a giant planet-killing machine. Is it worth risking the populations of Terza and Perpetra to save five people?"

He looked away. This was his nightmare. The worst case scenario. It had woken him several nights since the communiqué from the team had come through.

"Of course not. That's not my intention. Not at all."

She laid her hand on his arm. "I know it isn't, Temms. It's all right. It's a hard place to be in."

He drew comfort from the touch and the support in her warm tone. "So far, they don't realize we have this data, too. If we can find the thing, at least we're ahead of the game. Then we have something to negotiate with. At this juncture, I don't even know if we can find all three pieces. We have exactly one. This."

He gestured to the part, which Dani's team was now scraping samples of for analysis.

"You've got to admit, overall, this is the most random of the three. What are the chances that I'd meet up with Garrett Rawls, considering we're both from alternate universes? Strange."

She squeezed his arm, then let go, her smile returning to its former brightness.

"Seems like more than coincidence. Maybe it was meant to be, Temms. Perhaps you'll find a way to turn this back on them and defeat them."

"Maybe." He liked that concept. Perhaps it was actually true.

"Such a coincidence that Nik and I met Garrett, too," Valeni said. "But it's filled out our lives so much. He completes us."

The thought of blonde Nikki/Nicholas tugged at Temms' memory. The implications of a gender-shifting member of the crew who had one male and one female available suddenly settled in vivid focus.

Valeni laughed. "C.T. told us what happened when you met Nicholas. Poor you. We didn't realize you didn't know about him. But he really is a much better cook than Nikki. She can be a little scatterbrained."

Confused, he frowned. "What do you mean? Isn't it—he...um, she? The same person? Or maybe not even a person?"

"Not a *human* person. Each of the 'persons' have their own unique characteristics. Nik's of an alien race from the Rim somewhere. They'd learned to adapt to their surroundings by taking on whatever gender was necessary to survive. It's like those amphibians that are hermaphrodites and can reproduce even when all of them are ostensibly the same sex? But much prettier."

Temms thought about the sparkle in Nikki's eye. "Much prettier," he agreed.

"But back to this." She took a deep breath and let it out slowly. "I hope you'll meet with your council of mercenary captains before you make any final decision. What you do will affect all of us."

He held out his hand. "It's a promise."

She shook it warmly, and then pulled him close for a fragrant hug. "Thank you. We hold you and your hostage crew in our thoughts. Let's hope this matter resolves without having to even get to that point."

"Thank you," he said. "And thanks for bringing this. We'll keep you all updated on our findings. If anyone finds the other pieces?"

She stepped back and gave him a smart salute.

"You'll be the first to know."

He watched her walk out, the sway in her hips reminding him Garrett Rawls was a lucky man. A crew and friends that supported those in trouble were valuable assets. He was only now coming to realize his own wealth in that area. The independence he'd cultivated his whole career wouldn't serve him nearly as well as the community he'd now built. He had to trust in them and in his own ability to be a friend and companion. Right up until the time he could shove his retribution in the face of the Ancient and that smug Agent sitting on the station with his people.

CHAPTER 12

DELCIN stood at attention, waiting for Chief Agent and Commander Tuon Donn to disembark from his gleaming flagship, the *Arrow*. Donn had such presence. Everyone gave him an obscene amount of deference. Delcin wanted similar status so badly he could taste it.

The longer Delcin and his staff waited, he realized that Donn was toying with them. He'd keep the three rows of men and women in full uniform and arms at attention long enough to remind them who was in charge, and upon whose good graces they depended.

Considering the topics on hand, including Rogers' attack on the Primor'e office, Delcin would need every one of those graces.

He sucked it up and tried not to lock his knees. Passing out on the line would not be something that won points.

Finally, Donn's chief assistants came through the hatch and down the gangway, carrying stacks of data files and briefcases. A general wave of relief ran through the Agency personnel gathered to welcome their leader.

The ancient, still in his guise as sloppy, stout Jak Moster, hurried across the deck to stand next to Delcin, puffing as if this were actually his underexercised human body.

"I didn't think I'd make it," he wheezed.

Delcin eyed him a moment, wishing he hadn't made it at all. He'd hoped to have some time with Donn alone before having to deal with the acquisition of the station.

But if it wasn't for the station, you'd have no good news at all, right?

He forced a smile. "So glad you could make it."

Donn marched slowly down the gangway, his shiny black boots pounding loud enough to echo in the landing bay. His immaculate gray uniform bore a multitude of medals and commendations on the right shoulder. His perfectly-positioned hat sat atop a shaved head. There ended his perfection.

Donn's face was scored, upper left to lower right, by an ugly red scar he was said to have obtained in service of the Agency. His spine, too, was awkwardly twisted, causing an enormous hump behind his left shoulder.

Moster leaned close. "Doesn't the man have sufficient fortune to have that deformity repaired?" he murmured.

Shocked at first, Delcin couldn't reply. No one affiliated with the Agency would dare to question Donn, or particularly mention their leader's shortcomings. Donn himself proclaimed those flaws as further proof that he'd worked twice as hard as the others, overcoming these handicaps to succeed as the Agency principal.

But the question might be turned to Delcin's advantage. Anything to make himself look superior and the others crude and unworthy. "You'd have to ask him," he told Moster.

"Thank you, I will." The alien/man straightened his ostentatious red kerchief and awaited Donn's approach.

Not for the first time, Delcin wondered exactly how this being could be of a superior species, a race that had built this marvel of a station. He seemed fully incompetent to do just about anything except try to manipulate others into solving his problems. *Just as well we're going to co-opt this station out of his hands once it's functional. As inept as he is, he won't know how to use it properly. But we will.*

"My Lord," he said as Tuon Donn came to stand before him. "Welcome to the station. Allow me to present the Ancient who has invited us to join him here."

One of the aides leaned in, holding out a data pad for Donn's perusal. Donn frowned.

"This is Jak Moster, captain of the *Ramman*."

The Ancient stepped up inches from the Agency commander, his voice still in Moster jolly mode. "I have taken this form so I can work easily with you humans. It is much less threatening. To you."

Donn's eyes narrowed, but he was above all, a businessman. "How kind of you to make such a concession."

Moster beamed. "May I show you our station?"

The Agency commander's lips pressed together with annoyance as he surveyed the troops waiting for him, a scowl buried in his twisted brow. "I have many items on my agenda. I must first receive my report from Agent Delcin. Then perhaps a tour of the facility would be appropriate." He surveyed the bay, turning his shoulders to get the side views, his neck frozen in place. "What I have seen already is impressive."

Moster studied the men who'd disembarked with Donn. "Are

these new engineers? Problem-solvers to help decode the final sequences?"

Donn frowned. "No. These are my traveling staff, prepared to discuss Agency business while we are in this sector." He eyed Delcin. "Does this mean the station has not yet been made fully operational?"

Delcin swallowed down the bile that rose from his stomach. "Sir, we have made progress since my last report. Rogers' people discovered the parameters of the missing part, but the surveys to date have not located it on neighboring planets."

"So, not operational."

Donn's deadpan delivery sent a chill into Delcin's gut. *At least I have the possibility of the Bellonans.* "Perhaps we should discuss where we stand down in my office. I would be glad to conduct you and your staff there."

"Yes. We have much to discuss before we get to this latest failure."

Moster took several steps back, keeping his eye on the five men that waited for Delcin. "I'll be in the control room then. Please find me when you are ready."

Donn, focused on Delcin now, didn't even acknowledge the offer. Delcin sucked it up and took them down to his office.

Before he could even offer his guests refreshments, Donn took Delcin's own seat behind the desk. Donn's advisers took up positions along the wall, blocking Delcin's access to the door, and leaving him standing awkwardly in the middle of the floor, like a schoolboy called before the Prefector.

"Tell me, Agent Delcin, why is Temms Rogers a free man?" Donn asked, his fingers steepled before him, elbows on the desk.

"R-Rogers?" Delcin stammered. "I've concentrated on securing this station for the Agency." He tried to stand tall. This ought to be his proudest moment. He needed the extra confidence. "Besides, I've got his people. He'll be back. Then we can lock him up."

Donn didn't look impressed. "And how much damage can he do in the meantime? He and his ragged band of roustabouts?"

"But he hasn't—I mean, we haven't been informed of any activity since Primor'e—"

Donn's hand crashed, flat, onto the desk, causing a loud thwack that made Delcin jump. "*Since* Primor'e? Wasn't that enough? He caused damage in the five-figures and hospitalized three of my people! Or doesn't that matter to you?"

Before he could answer, Donn's steely gaze fixed on him. "This was your fault. You've mishandled this acquisition from the beginning. If you'd arrested Rogers and his co-conspirators after their terrorist attack, you'd have greater bargaining power over his crew. How long have you been here now? Three weeks? Four?"

Delcin had to acknowledge it. "Four."

"And the station still isn't running at full capacity?"

"We're making daily progress. I monitor every—"

"So, no," Donn said, voice flat and angry. "Please explain to me how it's possible that that fat little man can activate the landing deck and life support and still have no idea how to make the accursed thing useful?"

A question Delcin had asked himself many, many times. "He is assisting the decryption team, sir. Believe me, he has plenty of motivation to succeed."

"But no results." Donn leaned back in the chair, rocking a little. "What am I to do? You can't enforce the law, even when our own people are at risk. You can't produce a working station, even when it could solidify our superior economic power in this entire star system. You're nothing but a major screw-up, Delcin."

Donn continued to stare at him, and Delcin imagined that cold stare penetrating his clothes, his skin, taking the internal organs and freezing them one at a time, until it reached his heart and it solidified into a hard lump of ice and just quit working. His breath came in a gasp, and he got hold of his rampantly disassociating imagination. He was fine. He still had something to trade.

Taking a deep breath to reassure himself that all his parts still worked, he took a step closer.

"Were you aware that Rogers has a team of Bellonans aboard his vessel? A breeding pair?"

A warm, covetous light flickered in the Agency commander's eyes. "Breeding Bellonans? Outside the Consortium's control?"

"Exactly."

Delcin's chest loosened just a little. He recognized that look. It was the same one he'd displayed, certainly, when he'd coerced Williams into revealing the information.

"If we could get our hands on that team, we'd have one more advantage that the Consortium has held over us for so long."

Delcin nodded. "Another reason why dealing with Rogers has

been a slow, steady process, sir. With so many irons in the fire, I did not want to risk losing any opportunities."

Donn snapped his fingers and one of his aides slapped a datapad onto the desktop. He scanned it, read through a few pages of information, then turned back to Delcin. "So you have six of Rogers' people aboard?"

"Six in number, yes, sir, but one has already been converted to our side. A graduate of Sol Aeris."

Donn grinned suddenly, his scar twisting with the gesture. It was not an attractive move. "Ah, yes. That has been a very useful endeavor. So, five." He referred to his data pad again. "Three engineers, a navigator who is also first officer and—" His eyebrow tweaked with interest. "And Rogers' son."

"Yes, sir."

"It would seem you have plenty of bargaining material, Delcin. Get it done."

"Yes, sir."

"Don't harm the engineers, though. If anything, they're the only ones who may end up solving this riddle."

I'm not an idiot. "Of course, sir."

Standing in the middle of the room, all eyes on him, his nerves started to get the better of him again.

Donn eyed the pad again. "I see that your quarterly report is down nearly ten percent in collections from the expected projections."

That complaint, Delcin hadn't anticipated. "Sir, I've been engaged in arranging and capturing this station for the entire quarter, even after dealing with Rogers' little mercenaries' rebellion. Digging out the information on their activities—"

"I'm sorry, did I give the impression I wanted excuses?" Donn got to his feet. "Do you see me sitting here whining because I didn't get all the advantages the rest of you had? Not at all. I've achieved in spite of my so-called defects. You don't have any grounds to complain that you couldn't do this or you couldn't do that. You haven't complied with Agency directives and goals. Period. A penalty will be assessed against next quarter's earnings."

"But—" Delcin bit off his spontaneous objection before he could be further embarrassed. Not only was it pointless, but surely it would provoke further sanctions. "Yes, sir," he said, as calmly as he could.

Donn seemed faintly amused at Delcin's discomfort. "Now I'd

like that tour of the station."

The aides stepped aside and Delcin led the way out of his office. "I'd be glad to have my staff set up a meal for you, or at least beverages, if you'd like."

Donn wavered alongside him, his bone structure giving him an odd gait. "I'm sure I have better facilities aboard my ship. Don't bother."

Shut down again, Delcin bit his tongue to keep from saying anything else, his hands clenched into fists. Silently they proceeded to the control room, where they found the Ancient as well as Quinn and the oddly-striped alien.

As soon as Jak spotted them, he was immediately the gracious host.

"My dear Commander, how pleasant to meet you at last. This is the heart of our station, and we soon hope to have it beating at full strength." He went on, waxing voluptuously over the expected capabilities of the station once it was once again fully operational. "I'd hoped you'd bring some engineers or code breakers to help the process along."

Donn eyed the Ancient. "I was under the impression this process had already moved beyond the decoding stage." He glared at Delcin. "It is my job to supervise any acquisition of assets for the Agency, not to puzzle through the scut work myself."

Jak opened his mouth to speak again, then hesitated. He cocked his head, eyes narrowed. "I'm sorry. Perhaps I didn't understand you. Did you say acquisition of assets?"

"I did." Donn approached one of the consoles and slid a proprietary hand along its surface. "I'm sure our representative has explained this to you. In return for our support in getting this station up and running, we gain an ownership interest."

Jak stiffened and glared at Delcin, visibly agitated. "He never said anything of the kind. I've been attached to this station since it was first conceived. I've claimed it for my people, and I'm the only one qualified to use it to oversee this sector of space."

Delcin, standing deferentially behind Donn, had the opportunity to survey the deck. Both *Doubtful* crew members zeroing in on the conversation as if their futures depended on it. *Which of course it does.*

"Get back to work," he snapped, lashing out like a whip's edge.

Quinn glared, but sat back down at his workstation and at least made the appearance of trying to apply himself.

"The Agency does a fine job of overseeing this sector, and we really don't need the competition. Regardless of what Agent Delcin may have told you, an ownership interest is part of our standard transaction." Donn seemed unflustered by Jak's protest. "Of course, we expected to gain a share of something that actually functioned."

Jak eyed Donn with a burning gaze. "I think your personal situation shows that just because something works, doesn't make it pretty."

Donn's fingers twitched like they'd been hit with an electric shock. He turned his ruined visage on Jak, disdain dripping off his tongue.

"Are you insulting me? Because I assure you it's a waste of your time. I'm sure you couldn't come up with anything I haven't heard before, and certainly not something as original as the best of them."

Jak froze, less than two arms' length from Donn. His expression was a mask of horror and hatred. Such loathing emanated from his eyes that Delcin worried for Donn's safety. Donn's aides must have felt the same. They gently guided him backward to a safer distance.

Donn continued. "Delcin, why is it that you can't seem to maintain control over what happens in your own territory? You tell me that you have acquired new technology for us, but my initial pleasure is quickly dissipated when I see that you're working with idiots and fools, and that all we've gained is a hunk of fuel-consuming alien tech. This isn't producing anything that interests me in the—"

"I am no idiot, and I am certainly no fool!"

Jak quivered, and a bolt of lightning shot out from his hand, searing the uninjured side of Donn's face. Delcin leapt behind the nearest console, hunkering down behind its protection. From his crouched position, he could see that Quinn and his companion had done the same.

Donn's security man fired back at the Ancient, but a peek around the end of the console showed that his bullets had no effect on Jak. A faint shimmery field glowed around him, protecting him from Donn's retribution. One of the aides tended to Donn's burned face.

Donn himself was now shrieking at the Ancient.

"I'll tell you what you are! You're a dead man. I'll see that you're removed from this station immediately. My staff will take over, and we will be the ones who see success in this venture!"

The hair stood up on the back of Delcin's neck and his arms, and an electric tingle ran through his body. He could almost hear the crackle of the current.

Jak's defiant stare left no question as to his opinion of Donn, and by extension, his association with Delcin, too. Delcin could swear it appeared that the outline of Jak's body quivered and crackled, too. Jak leveled a hand at Donn.

"You are the one who will be removed. Alive or dead, it's your decision."

The security men fired again, but there was still no effect. Aides whispered furiously in Donn's good ear, and finally, he backed away.

"I'll expect you to keep to your bargain," he said. "It's how we do business."

The aides hurried Donn out of the control room. Delcin suddenly felt very exposed and alone. When he looked up, Jak stood over him. "I think there's some things you left out of our conversation."

At a disadvantage, Delcin stood up, now taller than the plump captain. He needed to re-establish his sense of control. Even with this new power to shoot lightning, Jak Moster had always been a mealy-mouthed pushover. *We just have to get back to where he needs me.*

"Perhaps we had a miscommunication, in that you were so eager for our help that you didn't listen to all that was said. I would be glad to go over the terms of our association again, if you want to follow me to my office."

"I do not intend to re-negotiate," Jak said in a voice thick with menace. "Neither do I intend to give up any part of this station. I have waited hundreds of years to have my opportunity to make this sector my own personal kingdom. Neither you nor your petty Agency will prevent me from doing so. Now get out of my control room."

Delcin floundered for potential retorts, but nothing came to him.

"We'll talk later," he said. He then beat a hasty retreat, wondering what he'd have to do to make this up to Tuon Donn. The Commander had been injured on Delcin's watch. That wouldn't be something easily forgiven.

But he was sure he could come up with something. Perhaps the Bellonan connection from Rogers. He had plenty of hostages to dangle over Rogers' head, particularly that annoying young man that was Rogers' son. Yes, that was it. He had to find some way to redeem himself to avoid derailing his career altogether. Rogers was definitely the key.

He returned to his office, his ambition and hope springing into action.

He would make his mark yet.

Just a little bit longer.

CHAPTER 13

ONE thing Benzi Quinn learned from his years growing up with an abusive father was how to tell the emotional temperature of a room. When it got just so hot, an explosion was right around the corner.

That was the current fever of the station control room.

Nearly twenty-one rotations after they had first entered the station to help the fake Jak Moster to secure the place, the *Doubtful* team had stalled just about as long as they could. In stolen bits of conversation away from obviously-monitored places, they'd compared notes and shared what they could. But it was coming down to the end.

The visit the day before from that blowhard Donn had kicked everyone from the Agency into high alert status. His threat to evict the Ancient from the station and take it over had spurred some real fireworks. The whole process had served as great amusement for Benzi, who sat back out of the line of fire and watched the Agency men get handed their asses as though it had been an entertainment hologram.

About time some of them got kicked around 'stead of us.

But when Donn had left, things didn't settle down. Still sizzling from the encounter, Jak had nearly fried Uri when he got underfoot, the poor kid left with third-degree burns across his shoulders. It took both Tommy and Benzi to hold Iov back. Benzi would certainly have struck back if Monty had been the one in the way. Dads stuck together.

Liang took the young wog off for treatment. The rest of them went uncomfortably back to work, giving the Ancient a wide berth.

Jak paced in the center of the control room for several minutes, then shouted at Benzi. "You! Come here. Now."

What in Sprechan's name had he done now?

Benzi glanced around his station, frantic to make sure nothing damning was exposed. Nothing he could see, anyway. He stood and then crossed the room, wondering just how far those lightning bolts could shoot.

Especially if the bastard realizes how much I do know.

"What you need, Cap?" he said, with as much calm as he could muster.

Jak scrutinized him with a gaze as bright as lasers, attempting to pierce his reticence. "You reported that you'd discovered the nature of the missing part. Is it possible that the device was disassembled and dispersed?"

Trying not to make direct eye contact that might be perceived as a challenge, Benzi shrugged. "I could see how that would happen."

"Show me a diagram of the potential sections."

This was the first time the Ancient had made a direct demand. The desperation behind such a move rattled Benzi's trouble meter.

"Back at my station—"

Jak grabbed his shoulder and shoved him into the chair Jak usually used. "Here. Now. Pull it up."

Aware he'd become the center of attention in the room, Benzi didn't resist the order. Instead, he entered his codes into the machine to unlock the file with the diagram he'd shared previously with both the *Doubtful* and the station personnel. "Now what?"

"Now we're going to find it. Or whatever part of it is local." Jak leaned against the side of the desk. "Have you determined the compounds that make up the *odahmeen?*"

He floundered for a good answer. It hadn't really been his objective to determine what the thing was made from. Too much digging in the station's records could have triggered an alarm, or let the Ancient know he was operating outside prescribed parameters. Instead, he'd sent the specs to Rogers. They could analyze it with less chance of discovery.

"Ain't it pretty much the same stuff that the rest of the station is made from?"

"You tell me."

He put on his most innocent face. "Cap, honestly, I don't know. I felt pretty good even finding the diagrams, considering I don't speak the lingo."

Jak stepped behind him, putting one beefy hand on his shoulder. "Fine. Then we'll take a look together."

Trapped between the alien and the console, Benzi could hardly squirm. "Sure, Cap. Whatever you say."

He punched in commands to manipulate the diagrams, turning the device to examine it from all sides. That hand rested like plascrete on his shoulder, an unneeded reminder that the Ancient stood much too close to screw around. He'd seen what the Ancient could do when angered.

Ain't my intention to become barbecue for no one.

Feeling a need to keep talking, trying to prove his worth, Benzi rattled on. "Looks to me like most of it's made of this gray metal here." He pointed out the hull of the thing, which matched the underside. "Rest of it's the same color, but see here, where the texture's different? I think this is made of something else."

"Yes, but what?" Jak snapped.

"Trying my best, Cap. See, if I had the thing here, I could test it, give you exact answers. You're asking me what a schematic's made of. It's not made of anything. It's just a drawing."

The Ancient's fingers clamped onto his collarbone like a vise, sending a painful jolt down Benzi's nerves, then they slowly released. He stepped away, hands trembling, then quivered, frozen in place. His outline shimmered, became bright. Only his eyes remained dark and focused. Then he regained the fat, jolly appearance of Jak Moster, going on as if nothing had happened.

"We must find it." He paced behind Benzi's seat. "This station, is it made of the same material as the so-called artifacts you had on your ship?"

That analysis Benzi had already done. "Some of them. Those that Captain Rogers had from the other universe, more like. The ones we gathered here, not so much."

"Where's that data?"

"Over on my workstation."

"Get it."

Almost afraid to move, that specter of his angry father hanging over him, Benzi climbed out the opposite side of the chair from where the Ancient stood and took the long way around to his desk. Iov met him there with a stack of data disks in hand.

"Did you see that?" Benzi whispered. "He—I don't know what in hells he did. Changed."

Iov nodded. "His energy resources are fluctuating. We had not previously calculated the amount of energy the Ancient needs to maintain a human appearance."

"Whatever happened with the Agency ducks must have drained him." Solutions raced through Benzi's mind. "Maybe we could suck him dry."

"It is worth considering." Iov frowned at the disks. "Will you give him the answers?"

Benzi sorted through them, replying in the same hushed tone. "Don't look like we've got much choice, friend. It's about to hit the fan, wouldn't you say?"

The Muuvo's dark eyes studied him. "What use will we be to the Ancient once he has the information he needs?"

The chill in Iov's voice echoed along Benzi's spine.

"Guess it's just another hand in our *abril* game, right? We play the cards the best we can and bluff when we have to."

"Enough talking!" the Ancient barked. "I want answers now!"

Benzi winked at Iov and then selected two of the disks. "Here we go," he said a little louder, and he returned to the anxious Ancient.

Reseating himself, he slid the first of the disks into the port. Once it loaded, he scanned to the chemical analysis. "All right, Cap, not to worry." He displayed the information in large font so it could be read over his shoulder. "Pretty much same as what you have here."

"Very well. Scan Terza for this chemical signature."

The enormity of the task made Benzi twitch. "Excuse me? The whole planet?"

The Ancient stopped his pacing, within arm's reach of the engineer. "Is there something wrong with your hearing?"

"No, sir, there ain't. Just so you know, it's gonna take time to do that. A real long time."

"Then the sooner you begin, the sooner you'll finish. True?"

The Ancient's voice relaxed, sounding almost light-hearted again. But there was no hint of amusement in his eyes.

"Guess it's true, sure." Benzi shrugged and entered the search coordinates.

"We've got several consoles here we can dedicate to this search," Jak said suddenly. "All of them. You," pointing to Iov, "and you," pointing to Tommy Rogers. "I want you to help him. Participate in the search."

He broke into a grin. "I know, we'll make it a contest. The first one to locate the *odahmeen* gets to go back to the *Doubtful* immediately. Won't that be nice? Come on now, I'm sure you're ready to go home. All you have to do it find this device's signature on Terza."

Tommy got to his feet. "But what if it's not on—"

"Then we'll scan Perpetra. And the next one. And the next one.

Until it's found."

The Ancient's smile faded.

"And if it's not found within the next 72 hours, then we'll start drawing straws to see who's never going home."

CHAPTER 14

"CAPTAIN, Agent Delcin is calling from the station."

Temms felt ice rise through his blood. He could guess from the veiled references his people had sent that little progress had been made. He was pretty sure that Delcin's call came as an announcement of negative consequences for that lack of movement: a death sentence for one or the other of his people on the station. Who would he find least useful?

Perhaps the Muuvo Uri, being just a lad in their accounting.

Or maybe Tommy's temper had boiled over once too often.

"I'll take it in my office," he said. Reluctant to face further failure, he pushed himself out of his chair, physically straightening his shoulders to make them maneuver in the direction he needed to go. The eyes of the bridge crew burned curious holes in his back as he stepped into the hallway that led to his office.

Once there, he took a deep breath to force calm. On the off chance Delcin had good news, he certainly didn't want to look weak. He rolled his head to the left and right, loosening tense neck muscles and sat straight in his chair. The pad and stylus lay on the left of the desk. He moved them to the right, lining them up parallel to the edge. He set the empty cup he'd left earlier on the floor, out of sight. A final deep breath, then he was ready.

He hit the button to route the message to his desk, and set the feed to video. "This is Captain Rogers."

The Agent appeared comfortable in his bright-white borrowed office. Delcin's uniform was spotless. And was that a smile? Not his usual assured, superior smirk. What was going on?

"Captain, kind of you to take my call. I thought perhaps we could talk business."

"Business," Rogers repeated, letting himself consider the implications. "I'm not sure we have much to talk about, unless it involves the release of my crew."

Delcin's lip twitched, but he kept smiling.

"I wish I could offer you that at this juncture, Captain, but as you know, we still haven't deciphered all the necessary records. I'm afraid I need their help a little longer. At least most of them."

Most of them? What did that mean? Anticipation spilled over him. Could he get some of his people back?

"I'm listening."

"Perhaps we can negotiate a trade. I'd be willing to release your son, in exchange for one or more of the Bellonan security shifters. Even one of the young. Preferably one of the young, actually. Or a pair." The smile firmed up again. "I had no idea you carried a team on your ship. Very clever of you to get your hands on them."

The hope that had sprung up when Delcin started talking faded quickly, leaving his insides cold. Temms would go a long way to rescue his people, but he would hardly trade off other members of his crew. A vision of Aronka telling Delcin face to face exactly what she thought of his offer to take her children brought a little satisfaction, anyway.

"That's a fascinating proposition," Temms said. "I'm surprised you're interested, with the crack security teams already at your command."

Delcin eyed him, lips pressing into a white slash. "We haven't forgotten about your attack on Primor'e, Captain. I've been able to hold off a retaliatory strike so far, as long as we're getting your cooperation at the alien station."

Almost laughable, considering how I fought off the ships on the way back from that incident. What's he really up to?

"Right. The fact that we can easily destroy your vessels has nothing to do with it, I'm sure."

The Agent growled and got to his feet, leaning closer to his monitor. "Do you tempt me, Rogers? I highly doubt you could withstand a full-on attack from *my* ship."

Temms leaned back in his chair and gave a little shrug. Delcin's ship likely had tech from Burko's stores, considering their earlier association. So the ships could be on an equal basis. As much as he'd like to crush Delcin's raging ambition, it would detract from the attention he needed to focus on his people. He chose a long, silent stare.

The Agent shifted in his chair, glancing away, then back at the screen. His growing discomfiture prodded Temms to go on.

"So you're looking to have your own herd of Bellonans, something to compare with the Consortium's numbers. Is that right?"

"Certainly that would be attractive. I don't intend to debate my strengths with you." Delcin's affable front had crumbled. "The deal's on the table. Take it or leave it."

Temms stalled, trying to avoid shutting down the conversation. Perhaps there was something else he might be able to barter. If he could get Tommy back. "I'll have to discuss this with them. Unlike the Consortium, I treat them as individuals with rights, not property."

Delcin's eyes widened just a little. "Really? How inconvenient."

Temms shrugged. "That's the way we do things where I come from."

"Very well. I'll give you some time to make arrangements. Let me throw another factor into your deliberations." He leaned forward, elbows on his polished desk. "Young ensign Rogers is the least valuable member of the decryption team. In fact, he's mostly useless, and he's beginning to cause a good deal of trouble. I'd guess if he's not removed from here soon, he's bound to cross the wrong man."

The smirk appeared.

"I'd hate to see him on the wrong side of the airlock."

"I'll let you know my decision." Temms said, ignoring the deliberate attempt to provoke him. He cut off the transmission with the stab of his index finger.

Hot fury surged through him that someone would callously use his son as a bargaining chip, followed by a cold rage at his own helplessness. He was in no position to storm the station, even with the other captains by his side. Any such attempt would surely cause the death of those held by the Agency. He couldn't appeal to the Ancients, not after they'd tricked him with Jak's imposter. All he could do was play along and try to find the rest of their damned artifacts.

For now.

CHAPTER 15

THE morning of their audience with the Lumina, they took their slipcraft down to the surface, their transport scanned and surveyed multiple times before the final landing. The delays caused Monty to fidget even more in the rear seat of the craft. Dani was hard-pressed to keep him occupied with a bag of small artifact pieces she'd brought along.

"It won't be much longer," Temms said. "I gave them the altered guest list days ago."

"The sooner, the better," Dani said, her normal good nature a little frazzled at the edges.

Temms studied his companions. Definitely not the guest list the Lumina had requested. Tasiq had left Gretta in charge of communication, and the Bellonans had pried Rey and Chandi away to Riviera's care. He'd brought Dani along to ride herd on Monty, who seemed more restless than usual in leaving his routine.

I still don't understand what need the Lumina has for Monty.

And I sure as hell miss Liang and Tommy.

And Hal.

A wave of regret whooshed through him with the memory of his lost friend and colleague. Months now, since he'd passed, but every so often, Temms still found himself expecting to walk into engineering and find the burly biped dissecting some piece of machinery at his usual steadfast pace.

But he had what he had.

Perhaps his predicament would be made more evident by the missing crew. He needed the help of the Lumina to make it possible to search for the *odahmeen* on Consortium lands. Arlen's carefully-cultivated disinclination to provide information had demonstrated there was no use in approaching him for more specific help. The Lumina's almost-enthusiastic response to his request gave him at least a little hope he might succeed.

Determined, he set the craft down in the space designated by the Consortium flitters. "Here goes nothing," he muttered.

Tasiq unfastened his safety belt and stretched. "Do you really believe that child has the power to help us? What I remember of her was a spoiled brat."

Seated behind the captain, in her human guise, Aronka growled softly.

"What you saw were the Lumina's last days of childhood. In the two solars since we left her, she will have undergone a transformation into a young woman fit to command the council of the Consortium."

"I imagine the financiers control the real power, don't they? "Temms asked. "Above all, the Consortium is an economic entity."

"True," she replied, "but the society constructed the form of government that places control into the hands of the council, and the ruler of the council is chosen from one of the families of power, sharing in rotation. The Lumina was destined to rule from the day of her birth. The traditions of the people are always followed, coming from far back in the history of this planet."

Tasiq's feline rolled r's became more pronounced with his excitement. "Perhaps the rebelliousness we saw in her when we once met will work in our favor."

"That would be a happy change of our luck." The captain got to his feet, his attention drawn to the rear hatch, where Dani knelt down, trying to hold onto Monty, who was struggling to get out, near-frantic.

"She's here! She's here! The Bright One!"

Temms hesitated to open the hatch, afraid Monty would burst out and disappear. "What's he talking about?"

"I have no idea! He just went off." Dani tried to calm the boy and get his attention. "Come on, honey, please, settle down so the captain can open the door."

"Where is she? I need to find her. That's what the dreams said."

More dreams? Temms had never thought to ask Monty about messages from the Ancients. In retrospect, though, Monty had been as closely involved with the Ancients' artifacts as anyone else. Perhaps he was the most logical choice. Temms studied the boy, now agitated and reaching for the hatch. Experience dictated it would be useless to try to gain any helpful information while he was in this state.

"All right. Someone hang on to him. We can't wait any longer if we're going to meet our appointment time. Anything we can do to earn the Lumina's favor will help get our people home."

Dani wrestled with the boy, but ended up getting socked in the face. She stumbled back, and Tabio stepped in, wrapping one strong arm around the boy's waist, Monty's back to his front. The child screeched and squirmed and kicked, but he was well-caught.

"Proceed, Captain," Tabio said.

Temms opened the hatch, and Tabio hurried out to clear the path for the others. Aronka helped Dani to her feet.

"You okay, D?" Temms asked.

"Eh. Had worse in a bar fight, I think." She rubbed her cheek. "At least he didn't break my nose."

He took a deep breath. "Then, let's get on with it."

They proceeded to the security checkpoint outside the main government building, their entrance ritual as stringent as before, first checking identification papers, then each member of the part had a drop of blood taken to verify genetic identification. Snipers watched over those coming from the spaceport. If any of them were not who they claimed to be, Temms imagined they wouldn't leave this square.

"You'd think after we'd done business with the Consortium multiple times, that we could get a pass or something, so we wouldn't have to jump through these hoops," he said *sotto voce* to Aronka.

"That is precisely the reason for the close scrutiny. Who better for criminals to impersonate than one who is trusted by the Consortium?"

"I guess."

The guards frowned at Monty's antics. "Why would you bring such a disturbed child to an audience with the Lumina?" one asked.

"Maybe you can ask her that. I have no idea. She's the one who requested his attendance."

The guards exchanged looks just short of an eye roll. The gesture lifted Temms' spirits.

So our little Lumina is a bit of an unpredictable element. I like this already.

When they tested the Bellonans' blood, an alarm went off on the machine.

"These two are not permitted on Consortium ground," the guard said. "Orders of Prince Arlen."

Aronka twitched and started to speak, but the captain, already annoyed by the overbearing measures taken, interrupted her. He stepped up eye to eye with the guard. "Again, *sir*, this is a question you'll need to discuss with the Lumina. She specifically requested that they come to this meeting." He crossed his arms and glanced at the communication device on the guard's belt. "We'll wait."

Not looking away, the guard did exactly that. He punched in some code, then waited for an answer.

"This is Tujal, at checkpoint sixteen. I have Bellonans here who are on the no-entrance list...Yes, sir. Verified...Mmhmm. I'll send the data." Fidgeting while he awaited the results of his query, he continued to eye them all as intruders.

Dani managed to get Monty calmed enough he'd hold her hand, standing next to her. The boy continued to speak in a soft sing-song tone, with references to "her" and "The One." Temms left well enough alone, not wanting to stir the kid up again. *Maybe I should have taken 'Lani up on her offer of drugs...I might use some too.*

Finally the guard received a message back. His face went sour.

"Very well, Captain, they are permitted to enter, but you are in charge of them and responsible for their whereabouts. They shall not leave your side, is that understood?"

"Of course." He made an ostentatious show of checking his timepiece. "Do we need to keep the Lumina waiting any longer?"

The guard gestured to his fellows to step back, except for one. About Tommy's age, the white-haired man stepped forward, dressed in immaculate purple livery trimmed in gold. His boots were almost shiny enough to generate a reflection of the group before him.

"I am Jahn," he said. "Please follow me."

He led the little group inside, issuing directives in an obsequious tone.

"Please remember when you speak with the Honored One that she is deserving of the greatest respect. You must not raise your voice to her. You may not ask her for—"

Aronka growled.

He glanced over his shoulder, face pale. "Y-you have b-been accorded a great privilege to be allowed to address the—"

Temms took pity on the servant. "Listen, son, we've met the girl before. We know how to deal with her. Thanks for the warning."

The young man stumbled, stopping to eye Temms in disbelief. "She can have you jailed for your disrespect."

Temms grinned. "Yes, but she won't."

Jahn stared a moment more, unnerved further by the soft sounds of amusement that came from Temms' companions, then stiffened. "Follow me."

The high-ceilinged, shadowy halls they passed through were

alternately paneled with polished dark wood and heavy deep purple curtains trimmed in the same gold braid as Jahn's uniform. Liveried servants carried showy arrangements of fresh-cut flowers past them, bound to decorate some corner of the residence. Thick brown carpeting swallowed up the sound of their footsteps. The occasional window showed a glimpse of vast lawns, a tall white gazebo, and fields beyond.

Finally, Jahn paused before a huge set of double doors of polished dark wood, fitted with gold fixtures. He knocked three times.

His heart pounding with the depth of how much he wanted this, Temms turned to survey his group. Even Monty watched the door, breathless. *We all have our hearts set on this plan's success. Surely we can't fail.*

The door opened from inside. The broad shoulders of a black-uniformed guard filled the doorway.

"Captain Rogers and his crew from the *Doubtful* to see The Honored One," Jahn said.

The pale blue eyes of the guard studied those waiting as if they might be poisonous insects, then stepped aside. "Enter."

Jahn preceded the team into the chambers of the Lumina, moving to the right, out of their path, once they were all inside.

Temms focused immediately on the young woman seated at the broad mahogany table. Aronka had spoken truly. This was not the same girl who'd ridden with them only two solars before. She was still as slender, her hair still as blonde, coiled in braids on her head. But those violet eyes had aged. She had an air of leadership and confidence about her.

Before he could speak, she stood, her lips curving into a smile, and spoke aloud.

"Welcome, Captain Rogers. I am pleased to see you again."

He'd expected her telepathy. From the startled look on Jahn's face, apparently it must be a special gift to be addressed directly by this young ruler.

He bowed in response. "Thank you for seeing us. Your new position suits you well."

"I trust I will fulfill my duties as required."

Her gaze flitted over the others in the party. She spoke in a strange language, looking at the Bellonans, and they bowed their heads respectfully and replied. Monty peered out from behind Dani, and the Lumina's gaze froze.

"It's her!" Monty gasped. "The Bright One."

Temms turned to see what he was talking about. *He means the girl. He's dreamed about her? What the—*

"What do you mean, love?" Dani asked, but he was out of her grasp before she could stop him.

"It *is* you," the Lumina said. She started out from behind the table. The guards immediately moved to block Monty from her.

"Your Eminence," Jahn said, his voice tight with concern, "this child has proven nearly uncontrollable since he's stepped on Consortium grounds. Please, do not endanger yourself."

Dani moved forward, reaching to protect Monty from the guards. "He's not going to hurt her."

Temm saw the opportunity to make his case dissolving in front of him. "Tabio, get him!" he barked.

All of you, calm down!

The Lumina's thought-command carried such power that it rocked Temms back on his heels. The others recoiled as well, the guards and Jahn both stepping back to the walls. Only Monty seemed unaffected, his youthful face lit with such joy it could not be dimmed as he reached out to her.

She hurried around the end of the table and took his outstretched hand. When they made contact, an actual glow came from the two of them, almost like an electrical connection had been made to complete a light circuit. They looked into each others' eyes, lost there as though they enjoyed a silent conversation that none of the rest could experience.

Baffled looks passed among the *Doubtful* contingent. Neither Tabio nor Aronka seemed to have more of an explanation available to explain the odd exchange. Finally the Lumina turned to the group, Monty's hand still in hers.

"I know you must be curious," she said.

Monty grinned, in an almost relaxed and natural fashion. "Of course they are." He looked at each of them, head to toe, as if he were seeing them for the first time.

Still confused, Temms looked from one to the other of them. "Agreed. And the answer is—"

"Tradition, Captain," Monty said.

The echo of the Bellonan's earlier words pulled at his stomach. And Monty's voice tone and speech pattern was almost that of a normal child. What was happening? He crossed his arms and waited.

The Lumina gently tugged at Monty's hand. "Let's sit down. Jahn, bring refreshments."

She retreated behind the table, seating Monty next to her. The guard pulled up other chairs to the table for the rest of them.

Jahn hesitated, checking a band on his right wrist. "Your Eminence, you have another appointment in ten minutes."

"Cancel it."

"But—"

She stared at him. Temms couldn't tell whether she was thinking words at him or not, but his respectful opposition suddenly folded and he bolted from the room.

Her face continued to hold that gentle smile as she studied the boy. "I always wondered what you looked like."

The captain frowned. "You know each other?"

Tabio sniffed the air. "We should have known." He turned to Temms. "They are of the same blood."

"Same blood? You mean related?" Temms eyed the boy. "He's of the Trellanan family? Prince Arlen's line?"

"We're twins, Captain," the Lumina said.

"What?" Dani sputtered. "How's that possible? If you're brother and sister, why would we have found him castaway on the Olesian reservation, starving to death?"

Monty smiled, a shy gesture, one very unlike any expression Temms had ever seen him make. Meaning swelled behind it, and intelligence. He and the girl continued to hold hands. "It is the way, Captain Rogers. Tradition."

The Lumina took a deep breath, glancing away for a moment. "It is something that outsiders might find hard to understand. If it had not been destined for our family to offer the next Council leader, a set of twins might not have mattered and we could have grown up together as brother and sister. But only one can rule."

She leaned back in her chair, still holding tightly to Monty's hand, gently chewing her lip. "I have only discovered this piece of family history in the last year as I've studied for my coronation. My parents' scientific advisers recommended that one of us be chosen to rule. After observing both for our first year, they believed that I would be better suited for the seat, as I was more verbal and social. Bena, the one you call Monty, seemed to have more technical talents and preferred not to associate with others. The scientists were able to mindprint some of his strengths and implant them in me, so I have the best qualities of both of us."

The engineer was still not willing to let this go. "So they sucked his traits out and then discarded him like last week's garbage? Do you have any idea what condition this boy was in when we found him? I can't believe Prince Arlen would allow something like that to happen."

"It is not a matter of choice. It is the law."

Temms didn't find the explanation particularly satisfying, and he could see Dani didn't either. As much as he objected to such treatment of a child, however, it wasn't his culture or his business, really. Protesting Monty's condition didn't get any of them or his mission farther ahead. Besides, the boy actually seemed better while he and the Lumina were near each other. So perhaps they'd achieved a remediation of the problem already.

The Lumina paused as food and drink was brought in. Plates were shared around, beverages poured, then the servants removed themselves from the room. The Lumina dismissed the guards, too, instructing them to wait outside.

"I must speak to my guests of important matters," she said. "I am in no danger with Aronka and Tabio here."

The guards glared at the Bellonans, but followed her orders.

"Please, everyone, refresh yourselves," the Lumina said. "I'm sure my rebellion will be reported, and we will get a visit from my Chief Counsellor well before we want to be interrupted." Her eyes twinkled with amusement.

She released Monty's hand, and the boy started to eat. She took a delicate bite of fruit. Her gaze flitted from one of them to another. A smile came when she reached the Bellonans.

"I apologize for not having your favorite treats to serve here—I take into consideration the sensibilities of the humans."

Tabio chuckled. "Watching us consume live prey isn't particularly appetizing."

Dani's hand hesitated over her plate. "Ugh."

"It's what makes us good at what we do," Aronka reminded her.

"I do miss you," the Lumina said. "I wish you hadn't left Grandfather's service." She sighed. "But I understand why you had to."

They nodded to her respectfully. "We have found the happiness we hoped for. We are most grateful to Captain Rogers for accepting us into his crew."

"As am I," she said, giving the captain a warm smile.

Temms allowed himself to relax a little. Perhaps his estimate of the new Consortium ruler had been accurate. She might be willing to work outside the rules to help them achieve their objective and locate the Ancients' parts.

"If I can tear you away from this long-awaited reunion...."

She laughed softly. "I have showed Bena how to communicate directly with me. You and I may continue our conversation. You seem quite troubled, and I've noted that your delegation is missing several of those I expected to see. Something has gone wrong in your travels."

He nodded. "We come today seeking access to Consortium lands to find some machine parts belonging to the Ancients."

"Who are these Ancients?" Her attention focused on him intently, giving him the impression that he might be the only man in the universe at that moment.

"We have encountered them only a few times in our travels," he said, giving her the history of the artifacts that had brought them to this universe, as well as those that had saved them in the battle with Burko, and then an update on their current status. "We had thought these beings to be benign and helpful until our encounter with the Ancient in the space station. Now that he has aligned himself with the Agency, they continue to hold my people."

She studied the pale golden liquid in her stemmed glass. "These are perhaps a race we call the Genarius. I learned about them in my history classes, as they interacted with the Consortium many, many years ago. But we believed they were dormant, or perhaps had moved on to another time and place." She tapped a finger on the side of her glass, thinking. "It is troubling to hear of them taking negative action. My study had showed them to be a positive force, as you had said."

"Unfortunately, we didn't learn the truth about this individual until it was too late. All attempts to gain entry to the station have been rebuffed, so we're at an impasse."

"I'm not sure how you believe I can help."

"We don't intend to trouble you. All we need is your permission to search Consortium lands for the potential source of such an artifact." He nodded to Tasiq, who slid a datapad across the table.

Unsmiling, she studied the data. "This is the specific description of the items you're searching for?"

"Yes."

"I will do my best to pinpoint the location for you from Consortium records, but if I cannot, I will certainly allow your teams to search directly." She eyed him curiously. "I take it, you have asked the Consortium for permission to seek this device?"

"I did."

When he didn't continue, she chuckled. "And they said no."

He shrugged. "I'm sure that's tradition, too."

"My grandfather is quite cautious and, shall we say, conservative, in his decisions." She smiled fondly. "Do you know what will happen if this artifact is assembled and activated?"

"Not exactly," Temms confessed. "The Ancient had said to me that the device would help the Ancients mix with the people of the universe and bring them a wonderful gift. Some great power would be released once the parts were found and the device completed." The betrayal of the Ancients killed his appetite and he pushed his plate away. "But in light of the actions of the one on the station, we must assume that his motives aren't pure at all. The machine may destroy everything. We have no way of knowing."

"And no reason to trust him at this time."

"Exactly. But we can't get into the station, and negotiation has proved fruitless. Until we can come up with another plan, we're preparing for the option that we'll have to comply with their demands."

Her expression took on a more adult look. "But perhaps you will not have to actually provide these parts to them. I think you'd agree that a station fully operational and armed might be a danger to us all."

"I would definitely agree, but as I said—"

"There may be records in the Consortium history that speaks of this station and these Ancients, as you call them. I shall have my historians look into this at once."

Temms cocked an eyebrow. "Not that I don't appreciate the help, but I'm guessing from Prince Arlen's response that the Consortium doesn't want involvement with this matter. Doesn't that put you in an awkward position?"

She studied him, then smiled. "I appreciate your honesty and consideration, Captain Rogers. From the moment we met, you have always treated me as an equal person, instead of some frightening dilettante. How could I act toward you any differently?"

Her understanding filled him with a warmth that had been

noticeably absent in recent days. "It's a deal."

"The official ceremony will take place in thirty days. I hope to have your information before then. As soon as we can, for the sake of your people." She glanced at the boy sitting next to her. "Would Monty be able to remain with me until you return for the event? I'd love the opportunity to come to know him."

"No!" Dani burst out. She grabbed the captain's arm. "You do remember that as a baby, they tossed him to the Olesians without so much as an instruction book and he nearly died? Or perhaps that was even the plan? If they discover he's here, will they finish the job they started?"

She eyed the Lumina. "I know it wasn't your fault, but for whatever reason, they chose you for all the goodies, taking all this away from him."

"Don't you see, Miss Dani, I am doing my best to make this up to him? If he's allowed to remain with me, I promise he will be treated with the utmost respect and dignity. He will come to no harm."

"So you say." Dani grumbled and stabbed something on her plate with a particularly vicious fork.

Convinced by Monty's odd reaction in the presence of the Lumina, his sudden relaxed state and his quick speech, that the affinity between them was an honest one, Temms leaned toward letting him stay, but he had to admit he had the same reservations as Dani. *If something happened to him before Benzi returned, I'd never forgive myself. And he sure as hell wouldn't forgive me, either.*

"What do you think about that, Monty?"

Temms studied the boy as he struggled to make eye contact. But when the Lumina took his hand, he suddenly straightened and smiled at them.

"I think it would be an adventure," he said. "I would like to stay with the Bright One. She is my sister. My real family." He tossed an apologetic look at Dani. "I do love my family on the ship. But I would like to meet the others who are of my blood." He shrugged. "If any of the artifacts are here, perhaps I can help find them."

Tasiq just stared in wonder. "Miraculous," he said. "His whole linguistic structure, his pronunciation, everything changes when they are in direct contact. I'm sure the doctor would like to study that connection."

The Lumina laughed softly. "As you can imagine, I'm not really at her disposal. Some facets of Consortium rule must remain secret."

Temms made a snap decision.

"I'll allow Monty to stay if Tabio can also remain." He glanced at the Bellonans. "Obviously I can't allow you both the time, because I don't know who'd manage your young. With the newborn, I'm assuming Aronka is more necessary on the ship."

"Babies?" the Lumina said, turning the conversation to the Bellonans' offspring. By the time they'd finished, the new young leader had agreed that Tabio could stay behind to keep an eye on Monty, with the understanding that if it became necessary, he could travel cloaked to keep her grandfather from finding out he was here.

"No sense in throwing gas on a fire, true, Captain?"

Things were going so much in his favor, Temms thought he'd roll the dice one last time.

"Is there any chance we'd be able to have a berth large enough to land the *Doubtful* at the time of the coronation, Your Eminence? I know you'll likely have many guests and less room than you'd like to accommodate them all, but it would be a blessing for the staff to be able to tend to some outside repairs and other matters while the rest of us share in the ceremony."

"I'm sure I can arrange that," she said. "It may be a way out of the city, but I can provide ground transportation for you."

"Very well."

Their meal concluded, and their business, too, Temms and his crew took their leave of the Lumina and the others. He personally gave Monty a communit, knowing the boy genius would know instinctively how to operate it if Quinn hadn't taught him, with strict instructions to call immediately if he had any trouble. On the way out, the Lumina ordered Jahn to provide Temms with coordinates of a landing berth. "Will two days on the ground be enough, Captain?" she asked.

He considered the stench on the lower deck. "I certainly hope so."

"Then I look forward to seeing you soon. Thank you for allowing Monty to stay with me. We'll have fun, I'm sure of it."

Dani's glare and the longing look over her shoulder as they walked away told the captain she wasn't entirely settled with the prospect of the boy's visit. But Temms believed the Lumina's promise to care for him. Who knew, he might even learn to incorporate some of her aplomb and speaking ability into his own nature, with the help of the scientists she'd spoken of. But they needed to get back to the ship. They still had much to do, and not much time to do it.

CHAPTER 16

LIANG was falling asleep at her console, and caught herself just before her head hit the monitor. She jerked upright and looked around for Moster.

No. The Ancient. I need to think of it as alien.

"Are you all right, Miss Liang?"

Uri's anxious voice at her elbow brought her back to the task she was supposed to be doing: scanning for the missing part. In the past three days, the team had already scanned all of Terza without finding anything that matched Benzi's chemical mix.

"Yes," she replied, with a tired smile.

"Are we going to find it?"

Uri's face held dark circles under his black eyes. He'd tossed and turned during their brief rest break, as she had. Knowing a death sentence hung over them didn't encourage closing one's eyes.

She wanted to tell him yes, to reassure him that everything would be all right. But after the drama of Tuon Donn's visit and the Ancient's struggle to maintain the illusion he was one of them, she wasn't convinced any of them would make it off the station alive.

"We're doing everything we can to search for it." She switched her review to a new part of Perpetra. "At least the Ancient has extended our deadline."

He handed her a disk to record her findings. "I'm sure everything will be fine, Miss Liang."

Now the children were reassuring the adults. What kind of crazy world was this?

She scanned the room to check on the status of the rest of the team. Benzi, Iov and Tommy all sat hunched at consoles, performing the same scans she was. Even Nim and two of the remaining Agency lackeys, part of Delcin's personal guard, had been drafted to scan for the specific metallic signature of the parts the Ancients wanted. Most of the rest of his cadre had returned to the ship, busy with orders Donn had left.

All the monitors had been tied into a master observation link watched by the Ancient, who sat apart from all of them, withdrawn. The last day or so, he'd had less and less interaction with them other than infrequent terse reminders to get on with the work. He seemed listless, only brightening when one of them logged a new find.

Uri followed her gaze.

"Do you think Benzi's right? That something is wrong with him?"

"Perhaps. He certainly seems to be weakening. The station remains at the same power level, so it isn't that he's drawing power from the station itself."

"Would he be stronger once the *odahmeen* is found and installed?"

"A good question." She rewarded him with a pat on the arm. "That may explain his desperation."

"Then why aren't we attacking him while he is weak?" Uri asked without looking up from his datapad.

Startled, she glanced at him. They'd seen what an angry Ancient could do. Uri himself had borne the brunt of an electrical attack. Brief snatches of conspiratorial conversation among the team had proposed various scenarios, but none had really appealed to them. The bottom line was that until they secured a way to escape from the station, attacking the Ancient didn't make much sense. When he recovered, they'd still be here. And they'd bear the cost of his wrath.

"We have to wait and watch, young one. Risking our lives without hope of success—"

"But what if there is no hope of success?" His impassioned voice was low, but hard as plasteel. "What if all we can do is assure that the station will never become activated? We can save those on the outside, if not ourselves."

Tommy glanced over at them, and she realized Uri's voice had carried. The last thing they needed was for this impulsive young Muuvo to spark an open confrontation.

"Hush, now. Our chance will come."

The Ancient stirred, his steely eyes zeroing in on Liang. "Is there a problem?"

"No. Please excuse the disturbance."

With a pointed warning glance for Uri, she set the program parameters to scan and stared at the screen again. Any positive result she found would appear on the Ancient's monitor. There was no way to hide anything any more.

It's definitely the final round.

The door to the control room opened and Agent Delcin stalked in, practically spitting with frustration.

"Look here, friend, I need my men back at their posts. You've got these scientists to search out your missing parts. There's no reason to compromise our operation here."

Liang stiffened at his impertinent tone. In its current state, the Ancient surely would not allow this to go unanswered. She moved her chair back to get a full view, curious to see what would happen.

The Ancient rose slowly from the chair it occupied.

"Your operation? Since when has your operation been a concern of mine? When you contacted me, you assured me that your crack team of experts could get my station running. But nothing you've done has brought us any closer to that goal. Your leader practically dismissed our efforts, in pursuit of my goals. All he wanted was to steal this station from me. These 'scientists' have at least made some useful determinations."

He walked across to stand facing Delcin. Though the Agent was inches taller than Captain Moster, the Ancient seemed to grow until he stood more than eye to eye with him. For the first time, Liang saw a hint of fear zip through the Agent's eyes.

"Well?"

Delcin sputtered. "We've kept Rogers out of your hair. We've provided security." He seemed to gather himself and straightened his shoulders. "You promised us useful technology. You've failed to produce anything of use. Frankly, if anyone here should be feeling deprived, it's the Agency."

The Ancient's jaw tightened and its body seemed to flicker.

"Look, Miss Liang!" Uri whispered, leaning closer, fascinated.

"I see it."

Was this the moment to attack, while the Ancient was engaged? She glanced around the room at the others, who were as transfixed as she.

She sensed something else was going on, though. *Perhaps we should wait.*

Delcin saw it, too, and took a step back.

"I have a better idea," the Ancient said. It turned and raised a hand. A bright current of light arced out from its hand, spearing the two Agency men. They jerked up from their chair, dancing in agony, then collapsed to the floor, smoking.

Tommy stood, but didn't move toward the Ancient. Benzi and

the others hung back, eyes wide.

"What in Sprechan's name is wrong with you?" Delcin shouted. He reached for the front of the Ancient's shirt, but the Ancient shoved him away. He flew across the deck, landing in a crumpled pile in the corner.

"I'm done with you and your people," the Ancient wheezed. The flickering was worse now, and he looked stressed. He waved his hand in the direction of the cargo/landing bay. "Your ship is banned from our airspace. I do not tolerate failure!"

It turned a glare on the *Doubtful* team and raised its hand again. Nim dashed across the room to step in front of Liang and Uri. The hand shook like a leaf in the wind, and then the Ancient discorporated in a flash of light.

Stunned at Nim's sudden gesture, Liang studied his face. "Is it you?"

"Liang, I—"

Delcin pulled himself up a console, rising to his feet. "Williams," he said, his tone cold. Nim froze, his face losing its concerned expression. "Come."

The Agent turned and marched out, and Nim obediently turned to follow him. Tommy crouched next to the fallen security guards, checking them for signs of life. He shook his head.

When they'd left, Benzi came out from behind the console where he'd taken refuge. "So is that it, then? Is he gone?"

Liang realized belatedly that the engineer spoke of the Ancient, not Nim. She and Uri joined the others in the center of the control room.

"I wouldn't count on it," she said. "It has very strong powers."

They stared at the fallen security men, the stench of scorched flesh pervading the room.

"So, what?" Uri asked. "He has to reset? Then he'll be back?"

"No," Tommy said. "That's not what's important here. The Ancient's dismissed the Agency. If their ship is out of the station's airspace, that means Delcin doesn't have troops at his command any more. How many does that leave?"

Benzi counted on his fingers. "Delcin. Williams. It's about time for their switchoff to next shift. Maybe there's not more than a couple of men down to Delcin's office. Who else stays round all the time? I think only the doc." His slow grin sparked hope. "Might be we could take 'em."

"Exactly." Tommy rocked onto his heels. "Now they're in the same boat as us."

Listening, Liang agreed with his thoughts. But her mind also spiraled off onto another track. Without the staff to prevent it, could she negotiate some way to have the doctor examine Nim and repair whatever the Agency had done to him? Her gut told her she was right about him. If they'd changed him, surely they could change him back.

"One less on their side, one more on ours," she murmured.

"What?" Tommy turned to her.

"We could get Nim back. If there really is a doctor aboard."

She explained her thought process. The others looked skeptical, at best.

"After everything he did, Liang, are you serious?" Tommy scowled. "That's not where our best efforts lie."

She drew herself up as tall as she could, her small stature feeling like a real drawback for the first time. "I'm the command officer here. I say we need to have as many on our side as we can get."

He eyed her, his blue eyes chips of ice. "And I say we take out as many Agency people as possible to even the odds."

They stared at each other, both stubborn.

Benzi finally broke the tension. "Hey, what say we find out how many are aboard for sure before we go all spit and piss, hmm? If we've got a doctor, then Liang can play with her pet security man while the rest of us get to what needs to be done."

Iov agreed. "Uri and I can go scout the station." He glanced up to where the Ancient had been standing. "If it comes back, better that some of us are still here working, so we don't end up like them." He nodded toward the dead men.

"Should we take them out?" Uri said, his eyes still wide and shocked. "I'm not sure I could work with dead men staring at me."

Tommy shrugged. "They won't get any less dead. If we've got a narrow window of time we have to take advantage of it now."

"How long do you think we have?" Liang asked Benzi.

"No telling. This is the first time he's been driven to vanish. I'd guess not too long." He stretched and rubbed a hand over his face. "But I'm also guessing now that he's shown his impatience and skills, he's not going to hesitate to go off on any of us who tick him off."

"True enough." Tommy eyed his console monitor. "Wish Jak wasn't able to scan these while we're working. We could be confabbing on what to do while we're just sitting around."

"I'll work on some kind of messaging," Benzi said. "But don't hold your breath."

"All right." Tommy straightened as if he'd come to a conclusion. "You two run along and check out the lay of the land. Stop in the quarters for a rest break on the way back, so you've got a reason for not being here. We'll keep at it."

Iov and Uri hurried out. Benzi ambled back to his station and plopped into the chair. Liang waited, torn as to what to do next.

Tommy put an arm around her shoulders.

"Look, Liang, I hope you're right. I hope for your sake that Williams can be saved. I mean, I like the guy. But if he can't, you've got to know that he has to be marginalized. We don't have a choice. If it's them or us—it's us."

She nodded slowly, looking up to find compassion now in his eyes. "Agreed," she said. "Now, let's get back to work."

CHAPTER 17

ORDERING Williams to guard his office door, Kile Delcin stumbled into his office, his world having just taken an oblique shift into unreality.

What had happened in there?

The accursed alien just fried his men like they were after-dinner snacks. Had it really cut him off?

He sat heavily in his chair at the desk he'd appropriated, a very nice desk. The nicest one he'd seen on the station. He ran his hand over its smooth surface, trying to find his ground again. *This is real. This desk is real. It sits here, and I can touch it.*

He took a deep breath.

What next?

Fall back on protocol. Contact the ship.

He dialed up his ship's frequency on his communication device, ready to order the second in command to blast the hell out of the station's doors.

Static.

He tried again. And again. Nothing but static.

He shoved aside the possibility that the alien had disintegrated the *Shelim* as easily as it had his security men. His ship was top of the line. He couldn't bear to lose it.

And what would Tuon Donn say about that?

Monumental failure sucking him into a mental vortex, he scrambled to stay afloat. Getting to his feet, he took measured steps, walking from one side of the room to the other, concentrating on the sound his polished boots made against the uncarpeted floor. The floor was real. He was alive. Perhaps the ship was intact as well, just cut off from the station, as Rogers' ship had been.

Which left him in the same position as Rogers' annoying crew. Powerless and at the alien's mercy.

Unacceptable.

He had to take action.

He had Williams. Who else? The duty roster showed him that

shift change had occurred while he was down in the control room. So most of his people on the station had returned to the ship. Those coming on duty would have debriefed them, then come aboard the station. *So they hadn't come yet.*

That left him seriously undermanned.

Damnation.

A rushed thought zipped through his mind that if his team and Rogers' team worked together they could defeat the alien. Remembering that lightning bolt of energy the alien threw at his men, he doubted that was true.

After everything he'd done to the *Doubtful* crew, he had to wonder whether they'd ever trust him enough to work together anyway.

Yes, he'd pretty well screwed himself.

He picked up his comm again and sent a local message. "Any Agency personnel remaining on the station, check in immediately."

Within seconds, he received a hail from the makeshift medical bay, two from the landing area and one from a tech down in the bowels of the station. He waited for more, but none came.

So, five including Williams and himself. At least that matched Rogers' team. Not a solid majority, but they were armed. That gave them a distinct advantage.

Facts clicking into place slowed the spinning of his mind. This was recoverable. It could be managed. He just needed time to think. And a drink.

He definitely needed a drink. The alcohol would calm the edges of his rattled nerves enough to let him think more clearly.

He dug in the bottom drawer of the desk for his flask, screwed off the cap and took a long slug. It burned all the way down, but he held on to that tingle, knowing it, too, was real.

No choice, he had to hold on. He'd sacrificed everything for this position of power, the rank of Agent in charge of the *Shelim,* one of the premiere ships of the Agency fleet. He had no wife, no children. He had not seen his parents in years. He'd betrayed friends, triumphed over enemies, moved heartlessly through the sector acquiring status, technology and wealth for the organization that was now his family and whole support. This was his life.

No frigging alien is going to take away everything I've worked so hard to earn. No way.

Strength and conviction of his rightness once again flowing into his veins, he summoned the remainder of his command to his office. Time to let them know their situation and lay their cards on the table.

Challenge accepted, you alien bastard.

* * *

THE Ancient stayed gone, and Benzi didn't mind a bit. Without the fat alien looking over his shoulder, he played with ways to communicate through the jamming the Ancient had placed on them so far. If they'd gotten through on a regular transmission with a piggyback, there had to be another way to make it happen. So far, he hadn't been able to devise anything that would allow them to send a message without being detected.

That was really more Iov's thing, but he hoped to use his special language skills to talk with the Ancients' computer and find a way in.

Liang scribbled furiously over at her workstation, using a stylus and plain paper. So clearly not something for the good of the Ancient. Probably her mission to un-brainwash that cocky ass Williams.

The fact she'd chosen the good-looking and muscular Williams over him did burn him a bit, but nothing like it would have a year before. Back then, a female's rejection always tied itself to his mother abandoning him for her New Peruvian lover. But now not so much.

The realization nagged at him. Why was it suddenly different? He remembered first arriving on the *Doubtful* and coming up with hateful limericks when Liang had rebuffed his advances. He even set his cap at winning her over then, just to prove his self-worth. But nothing had worked.

His da's voice came into his head.

'Cause you're never good enough, bucko. Allus be a river rat, never good enough for the likes of women of quality.

He closed his eyes and shut out that hated voice.

You're dead and gone, old man. I have people who love me now. I don't need you any more.

His heart wrenched as Monty's face passed through his mind. Was the boy coping with his absence? Was Dani caring for him, or had he regressed? He honestly missed the kid, even though he'd never expected to have someone depend on him that way.

Then there was Zandra. Her tentative overtures reminded him that others out there cared for him. He'd always been too busy to act on those impulses.

But if we get back to the ship, I'll not wait any longer. That I promise myself. It's time for old Benzi Quinn to become part of the world. I've got my ship, my crew, my boy—and just maybe a real chance at love.

The thought filled him with the most unbelievable joy. He felt the way he imagined Monty felt when he worked with the artifacts—that wide, beatific smile, soft eyes and relaxed posture just radiating contentment. He might have a few more things to prove to the damned Agency and this wayward Ancient. But as far as his own crew was concerned, he had showed them everything he needed to. Benzi Quinn had found a home.

A grin creeping onto his face, he turned his attention back to the message sending. Time to make that homecoming happen.

The Muuvos came back fairly quickly, arriving out of breath, looking anxiously around for the Ancient.

"What did you find?" Tommy asked.

"The doctor is here, as you guessed," Iov reported. "We found two men in the landing area, but they received a call and hurried away before they saw us. We saw no one else."

Tommy grinned. "Five and five. Sounds like good odds."

"If we can take out the security men, we could get their weapons," Liang suggested. "Then we should be able to force the doctor to perform the necessary measures for Nim."

Tommy stopped just short of rolling his eyes. "I'd rather make sure Delcin is neutralized. He's the one with the bite."

She chewed her lip. "Fine. There's two of us and two missions. We'll track down the men first, then split up."

"And just leave us hangin' here when old Moster decides to make his reappearance?" Benzi asked.

"We will wait with you, Benzi Quinn," Iov offered. He sniffed. "In the meantime, we can remove the bodies of—" He gestured over at the burnt corpses of the Agency men.

Benzi walked over to join them, speaking in a low voice. "It might be kosher to get a message to the Cap as soon as we can about the change in circumstances here. If they've got a chance to get in, it'll be a whole lot better as long as the Agency is out."

Tommy considered that. "Can we get an outside scan? See where everyone's ships are located? I mean, for all we know, Da—the Captain's off tracking down these parts the Ancient wants and isn't even close by."

Benzi nodded. "We haven't had that kind of access, but I may be able to hack into the computer the Ancient's been using. Bet it's all laid out there."

"All right. You do that. Liang and I will go see what we can do to secure the place and make sure we end up on top. Buzz me if something changes. Or if Moster returns."

Benzi glanced at Liang to see if she'd challenge the younger Rogers' authority, as first officer, but she just grabbed the papers on her desk and the stylus.

"You got it, sir."

Benzi wandered over to the console the Ancient had been sitting at, walking all around it first to see if he could feel any sort of presence there. It was odd that he had vanished like that, and Benzi had honestly expected a reappearance almost immediately. But it hadn't happened.

But he did get his first opportunity to thoroughly study the Ancient's work station, and its ostensible power source, which ran off a different feed than the rest. He wasn't quite brave enough to work on the Ancient's computer keyboard, just in case he came back, but he spent some time trying to break into it via the computer network, without success.

After Iov and his brother removed the bodies of the Agency security men, they returned to help Benzi attempt contact with the *Doubtful* or any other friendly ship outside, but they had no luck. Whatever device extending the invisibility cloak around the station, it continued to lock them down tight. They'd need special dispensation, like what Liang had requested the first time, to get them a free pass.

Don't think old Jak's gonna be in much of a mood to be magnanimous about such things at this juncture, I sure don't.

Flying blind was hard, no question. But all they could do was press on. The threat of the Agency had been considerably reduced. They'd found a chink in the Ancient's armor as well. Maybe with a little more faith and another roll of the dice, old Lady Luck would turn around in their favor.

CHAPTER 18

THREE days after their meeting with the Lumina, Temms Rogers got first wind that something wasn't right back at the Ancient's station.

Garrett Rawls pinged him by holocall from his bridge. He appeared on the large monitor on the *Doubtful's* bridge, lounging in his captain's chair, booted feet propped up on the nav station.

"Temms, buddy, wanted you to know something strange is going on. We're currently in orbit at Terza, but we can read the station on long-range. The Agency ship *Shelim* has pulled away from the location of the station, but they're sending shuttles and other flitters to try to breach the landing area. They cannot get in."

Was this a good thing or a bad thing? Temms couldn't decide.

"Any idea why?"

Garrett shook his head. "The Agency's frequency is scrambled and encrypted. Even if we knew what they were sending, we probably couldn't understand it." He leaned back in his chair, his attention caught by something else on his bridge.

Valeni moved up behind Garrett's shoulder. "Looks like the Agency may have suffered the same fate as your ship. The Ancients no longer want to deal with them."

"Hmm. If they're hanging around, I guess we can assume that some of their people are still aboard the station. No way of knowing how many, I suppose. Or who." He sighed. "Let's hope this means Delcin will begin to see reason, rather than it setting him off to do something stupid."

She shared a sympathetic smile. "There is always a first time. If we learn more, I will let you know immediately."

"Thanks for the information."

They signed off, and he leaned back in his seat, resting his head on the top cushion, eyes closed. So what did that mean? If the Agency had been deposed at the station, did Delcin remain alive? Did any of them? No way to know, and no way to find out. He was bound to stay here at Perpetra through the time of the Lumina's coronation, especially if she was intending to help him. The last thing he could afford to do was insult her. So he'd remain.

The Ancient would contact him when he needed to act, of that he was sure.

They sure as hell have had no problem disrupting my life any time they wanted something.

But at the same time, when they had previously intervened, it had been to help him, seeming not to require anything for themselves. He found it hard to reconcile those two attitudes. He'd worked with many difficult people over the years—heck, he'd made many of them into solid crew members. But nothing had been as inconsistent as these.

Certainly the Ancient who impersonated Jak Moster was aware of the actions taken by the Ancients who'd had contact with the *Doubtful* previously. But that didn't necessarily mean they were part of the same working group. Did it?

Before he could spend too much time pondering it, Tasiq announced over the comm that he had a call from Consortium headquarters. "The spokesman said it was the Lumina," he added.

That brought Temms fully intent. He set his tea aside on the edge of his black-surfaced desk.

The monitor came to light, one of the liveried housemen waiting for Temms to appear. When they made eye contact, he sat up straight. "Captain Rogers, the Honored One will speak to you now."

He moved out of the screen's view, and the Lumina came on. This morning she was relaxed, more casually dressed than at their formal meetings, her hair down around her shoulders. Her eyes sparkled with excitement. She spoke to him by the efficient method of telepathy.

Captain! I'm so glad to catch you at a free moment. I've had my staff hunting down the research we discussed. The records do indicate an alliance many, many years past between the Lumina of that era and those you referred to as the Ancients.

A schism occurred in the ranks of these Ancients, with some wanting to set the humans on a path of growth to let them develop without interference, and others wanting to use their superior powers to keep their hand in the ongoing progress of the emergent cultures.

Temms frowned. "Let me guess. The one in current possession of the station is one of the latter."

She nodded. *Those willing to protect humans took the power source and broke it apart, distributing it over several universes, as you suspected. When the others decided to try to recover it, they sent out artifacts to various universes trying to bring the exact parts they needed out of their hidden places.*

"So we have one part from Garrett Rawls' universe. I believe one of the artifacts we recovered from Kitana's collection will match part of the device. We have one yet to find. I don't suppose your research reports where one might be found in this universe?"

A brilliant smile spread across her face, and he realized for the first time that she was not only intelligent and gifted, but also beautiful.

Why, thank you Captain. That's very kind of you.

He blinked, surprised. "What? Oh." His face flushed. "I forgot, you can read my thoughts as well." Unbidden, the corollary crept through that he was glad he wasn't the father of such a woman, having to deal with potential suitors and other complications. Amusement in her eyes showed she'd caught that one, too. No way he was going to dig himself out of this situation.

She laughed. *I'm sure it is true, Captain. Perhaps that is why I must have a whole council of the Consortium to aid me in making those decisions.* She looked away from the monitor. *Tell them I shall be along in a few minutes. Leave me.* She waited briefly, then turned back to the conversation.

I don't have much time. Other duties call. But yes, we have tracked down a mysterious reference to the relic hidden in this system. Perhaps it means more to you than to me. She pulled a thick book close to her and put on gold rimmed glasses to read the page. *The Lumina of the Consortium agreed that her chief advisor would take possession of the remaining relic, hiding it where those malfeasants would not find it. It is hidden deep in the ground, in a series of caves. The gate to this buried artifact is guarded by fierce beasts who will take the life of a man in one swipe of its mighty paws.*

She looked up, leaving him hanging.

"And what planet is that?" he demanded, about to be frustrated all over again.

It does not specify.

He growled and rubbed his forehead, but when he rethought the description, the words came back to him, and resonated. Caves, and wild beasts. There was one place he knew that fit that description exactly. It was a place that lay far from the technological worlds that would be the most logical source of an artifact. The site was in fact, perfect.

She watched him with growing interest. *You know this place,*

Captain?

"I believe I do. Do you have coordinates or any other identifying evidence?"

Some other data was fixed to the bottom of the page. I'll send that along to you.

"Thank you, your Highness, for your assistance in this matter."

I still have concerns about removing these relics from their concealed grotto. We cannot allow them to fall into the hands of these Ancients.

"Agreed. That's not my intention. But I've got to at least have them, so I can get in the door to get my people. I promise, I'll keep my hands on them."

A buzz of activity occurred behind the pretty blonde girl, and Monty's head popped up on the screen. He laid a hand on his sister's shoulder.

"Captain! It is good to see you," Monty said.

Temms couldn't believe the change in the boy. His eyes were bright, his attitude charming. He seemed thoroughly focused and intelligent, a far cry from the emotionally distraught, mumbling child they'd dealt with here. "Same here, Monty. I want you to know we're doing everything we can to get your Da back home."

"I know. The Lumina has shared what you said with me."

Temms wondered if the girl was in telepathic contact with Monty, and decided it made sense. "So you're getting along fine there? You know you can come home whenever you're ready."

"Of course, Captain. Thank you so much for your kindness." He glanced at the Lumina, then back to the Captain. "All your kindness. Including taking me in when the Olesians abandoned me there. You didn't have to accept me, but you did. And you found me the best father, someone who understands machines and needs them, the way that I do. I am so grateful."

"You're welcome, son. I'd better go now if we're going to locate this part. If you need anything, call. Otherwise we'll see you at the official ceremony in a few days."

"Okay!" He disappeared into the background again.

He's been building things ever since he arrived. He's quite gifted. The Lumina smiled. *I owe you a great debt for reuniting us. I hope the information I've shared with you can be the first step in repaying what I owe.*

"Nonsense," he replied. "With what you're doing for that boy, I assure you we are more than even. Thank you again for your assistance. Rogers out."

He cut off the channel and sat back in his chair. Strange how life worked out. Things moved in circles. His experience finding artifacts here began at Lennor, and it looked like it would end there, too.

And then, Jak, I'm coming for you.

CHAPTER 19

LIANG slipped along the corridor, moving toward the section Delcin had appropriated for his command post, her feet hardly making a sound. Tommy followed close behind, weapon in hand. They'd made a sweep of the landing bay without finding Agency personnel, but it was a fair guess Delcin had called his staff in to regroup. If they were going to find anyone, it would likely be here.

She didn't fully trust the estimate of Agency people aboard the station, not because she thought Benzi couldn't count, but just because nothing was as it seemed, pretty much from the time they'd arrived. Everything remained unpredictable.

The sound of bootsteps came from the left corridor ahead, and Tommy grabbed her arm, pulling her to a stop. She released the annoyance at his assumption she didn't know how to behave, and backed up against the wall, waiting. Sure enough, two men in Agency security uniform came marching around the corner, stopping short when they spotted the *Doubtful* team.

She grabbed the wrist of the man closest to her, yanking him forward into the wall. He stumbled and she chopped at his neck, rendering him unconscious. Tommy had more trouble with his man, scuffling and wrestling to the floor, both of them roughed up before Tommy finally subdued him with a headbang to the floor. They dragged the two men to a nearby closet and tied them up with some electrical cord they found inside.

"Two down," Tommy said.

"Let's hope there's only two left." Liang stretched her shoulders back and straightened her jacket. "I'll take Nim."

Tommy shook his head. "If you insist. Once the door's clear, Delcin is mine."

She nodded and they crept up to the corridor intersection again. A quick peek around the corner showed her Nim stood guard. Remembering the bruises he'd given her in their last combat, she hesitated.

No, I have to do this. I have to know. Even if I have to knock him out and drag him to medical myself.

Steeling herself, she took a deep breath, then stepped out into the hallway.

Nim stared straight ahead at first, then he slowly turned his head in her direction. His lips silently formed her name.

Now or never.

She ran lightly along the corridor to meet him. Staying out of arms' reach, she studied his troubled eyes.

"I'm trusting that something has happened to you that you cannot control," she whispered. "I want you to come to medical and have the doctor check you out. If any part of you cares for me, you'll come with me."

Nim's foot moved, but he remained in place.

"I have orders to guard the door," he said.

She sighed. "Of course you do." Just her luck. It wouldn't be the easy way, apparently. Any kind of big fight right outside the Agent's door couldn't possibly be missed. What was she going to do?

"Hey!" Tommy called. "What's going on?"

Her heart sank as Nim turned in Tommy's direction. *Idiot! What did he think he was—Oh!*

Realizing Nim was now distracted, she kicked his arm, knocking his gun from his hand, then darted in to grab it, coming up to smack Nim in the left temple. As she'd hoped, he crumpled to the ground.

Tommy grinned. "You're welcome."

She made a face in his direction, then bent to try to hoist Williams onto her shoulder. He was taller than her by several inches, and as dead weight, easily nearly twice her bulk.

"Wait, wait," Tommy said. He ran up beside her and bent down to shoulder Williams himself. "Medical's not that far. Come on. I've got to get back before Delcin realizes he's gone."

He staged off down the hall in the direction of medical. Liang trailed him, Nim's gun still in her hand.

When they entered the medical office, the doctor turned, eyes wide. "What happened?" he said.

"Guy took a shot to the head." Tommy and his cargo blocked Liang from the doctor's view, till he plunked him down on the table. "Gotta go." He shimmied out of the room, and Liang put the end of the gun in the doctor's face.

"I don't want to shoot you, but I will," she said, her cold gaze hopefully leaving the medical man no doubt she meant what she said.

"This man is being controlled against his will. You're going to remove the device that's doing it."

"I don't think so," the doctor said. He took a step backward, his gaze scanning the counter to the side.

"I know you need your hands for the operation," she said. She aimed at the outside of his thigh and pulled the trigger. The doctor yelped, and a bloom of red appeared on the leg of his uniform.

"Do you know what's happened?" she asked. "The Ancient has cut you people off, just like it did us. You're at its mercy now, just like we are. The Agency security men are dead or locked up. We need all the people we can get at full capacity if we're going to defeat it. Fix him. Now."

She aimed at his knee.

He lurched sideways, enough to grab a thick piece of gauze to hold to his wound. "Even if it were true, how am I going to find such a device?"

Was he really innocent, or was he just buying time? Knowing Tommy had likely moved into Delcin's office now, she didn't have time to find out.

"Same way I will, I suppose, if I have to. Use the scanner." She fired again, slicing through his pant leg a second time. He stumbled and she leaned across the table, grabbing the front of his shirt. She jerked his face close to hers.

"I don't have time to waste. Another dead Agency man does not matter to me. Either do it now or I'll shoot you."

She released him, charging the weapon for another shot.

He glared at her, but pulled the scanner overhead into place, then activated it. She didn't dare glance at the scan results, but kept her focus on the doctor, watching for him to make a suspicious move.

"How do you know I won't just kill him?" the doctor asked, picking up a scalpel.

The gun barrel didn't waver. "That would not be in your best interest."

He stared at her, then finally capitulated. "Before I bleed to death," he muttered, turning Nim's head to the right. He cut carefully into the skin just behind the left ear, moving the flap aside, then taking a pair of tweezer-like instruments forceps to grab a shiny piece of metal about the size of a large fingernail. He removed the object with a tug, along with a small copper-colored wire that trailed from it.

She watched, holding her breath until she got light-headed. It was true. They had controlled him. He hadn't attacked her voluntarily. She hadn't made a desperate mistake of character. He would return to her.

Relief washed over her like a flood as the doctor stitched up the incision he'd made. Just in time, too, because Nim began to come to.

"Liang?" he murmured. "Where's Liang?"

"Right here," she said.

"What—what happened? My head h-hurts." Nim's arms moved feebly, trying to gain purchase on the edge of the exam table to push himself up.

"He should be allowed to rest," the doctor said dryly. "Although I don't suppose you'll listen to me on that point either."

With a tight smile, she extended a hand to Nim to pull him upright, the other still holding the gun. "No time. Sorry."

Nim stumbled to his feet, and she quickly tucked her shoulder under his arm, letting him lean on her as she backed away from the doctor. The doctor just waved her out, turning to the tray behind him for bandages for his leg. She didn't trust him, though, and didn't put away the gun until she was out in the hall and the door closed safely between them.

No one else was in the hall. She spotted the galley off to her right and made her way there with Nim's weight becoming less and less on her as he woke fully. She dropped him into a chair. His hand went to the side of his head which remained sticky with blood.

"What happened?" he asked again. "Did you hit me?"

"Ah, yes. But that's not what you're feeling. That's where the doctor removed the chip the Agency had attached to your brain that let them control what you did."

She studied him, still aware this could have been a voluntary thing on his part, despite the involuntary nature of his compliance. Was he complicit in his own mutilation? His reaction would tell her where they stood.

"A chip?" He stared at her, disbelieving. "How? *When?*" He leaned back in the chair as if hit by a huge heavy ball. "Did I do—oh, Sprechan's fryhole." His eyes got wide and he gaped at her. "Liang, I—I'm—I didn't mean to...."

He came out of the chair and took her in his arms. "I hurt you," he whispered into her hair. "I didn't mean to. I'm so sorry." He held her away from him, studying her face. "Are you all right?"

"I'm fine. Much better now." She wanted to remain standing

there in his arms, but the gravity of their situation nagged at her. "We should get back to the control room," she said.

He cocked his head, thinking. "Did the Agent correctly report that the ship's been cut off from the station?"

"Yes."

She was already moving toward the door. If the Ancient had come back to discover their absence, she didn't know how long Quinn and the others could cover their missing status.

"But the Ancient left. He'll be back, I'm sure of it."

"What do you mean, left?"

She took his elbow to get him moving too and headed back toward the control room. A random thought crossed her mind, wondering if she should stop to see if Tommy needed help, but she dismissed it. The cocky captain's son seemed confident enough to go it alone. She'd let him try it. Better to get the situation in the control room dealt with, now that the Agency staff was under control.

Just before they entered the control room, Nim stopped and caught her arm. He looked down into her eyes, his vibe finally warm and welcoming once again.

"Thank you so much for standing by me, Li. I tried to tell you, but I couldn't. I was sure Rogers would—"

She laid her fingers on his lips. "I heard you, doing your best."

He smiled. "It was all I could do."

She opened the door. A quick look showed her the Ancient had returned. Benzi's eyebrow raised at Nim behind her, but he kept typing, not drawing attention to himself. Uri and Iov both brightened as Liang walked in.

We haven't really planned this well. How will we let the Ancient know that Nim isn't an Agency man so he doesn't get fried?

Perhaps the best way to make that happen was to be straight up.

She stopped at her console, Nim by her side, to make the announcement. "The doctor found the chip in Nim's head and removed it. He's part of our crew again."

The Ancient wound up, as if to make a comment.

"He's here to help us," she added.

"Good. We're scanning Perpetra now." It eyed Nim. "You can use the console that young Mr. Rogers has been using." Its gaze turned to Liang. "I take it he's resting?"

I doubt it.

"Yes, I believe so," she replied aloud.

Suddenly, there was a dull explosion and the station shook.

"Oh, Sprechan's bleeding balls," Benzi said. "What's that?" He tapped on his keyboard. "Are you kidding me?" He looked up at the Ancient. "The Agency ship is firing on the station."

"They can't harm us, as your own Captain discovered. The station's shields will protect us." The alien turned an impassive face to the screens. "But if they choose to waste all their ammunition, they are certainly at liberty to do so."

"You're not going to shoot back?" Quinn asked.

"I have no need. Get back to your scanning. Time is running out on the *odahmeen*."

Liang considered the seeming contradiction that the alien would kill them, or Delcin's Agency goons, with little provocation, but when a real attack came, simply watched, blasé and bored.

So if we're going to stress the alien to the point of discorporation, it will have to be with incidents on board the station. We're not going to be able to rely on anyone outside to help.

"What should I do?" Nim asked.

She directed him to her station. "We're just scanning the planet now for the correct chemical signature. We have to find a part to activate the station's higher levels."

He looked at her in disbelief. "The whole planet?"

She smiled without warmth. "We've had that discussion, believe me. We've finished Perpetra, we're on to Terza. Then we'll get the outer planets."

"At least it buys time," he said in a soft voice.

She nodded. "That's why we're proceeding slowly and thoroughly. Very thoroughly."

"Understood."

Nim's presence handled, she turned her mind to the next problem: how to slowly draw energy from the alien until they could turn the tables on it? And fast. They only had so long they could keep the Agency people under wraps. She fired off a message to Benzi Quinn. If there was anyone in their little band who could manage to screw things up through trickery and technology, he was their man.

CHAPTER 20

DELCIN awaited his people in his office, but none of them ever came. He paged them over and over, each time they didn't appear making him more perturbed and more paranoid. Had the Ancient discovered a way to kill them from afar? How long would it be before it was his turn to face that electric death?

"Williams!" he called.

Nothing.

A growl burst from his tight throat and he went for the door. It opened as he approached, but it wasn't Williams standing outside. It was Tommy Rogers, carrying one of the Agency men's weapons.

The young man grinned. "Well, hello there." He shoved his way past Delcin, coming into the office.

"Get out." Delcin peered out into the hallway. No Williams. *What was going on?*

Rogers smirked. "If you're looking for your guys? They're gone."

Outraged, Delcin spun on him. "That alien?"

"No. Not at all. Me." He continued with that self-satisfied look, so like his father.

Delcin was tempted to grab a weapon from his desk drawer and sear that off his face. "What do you want?"

"I think we should talk, in light of the changed circumstances here. I know you were feeling superior and special, what with having a gunship off the bow and all, but clearly that no longer matters. Which leaves you in the same position as we are. Hostages of an unbalanced alien life form that apparently wants to betray every alliance it makes and rule the sector over everyone's objection. Sound about right?"

Rogers plopped down into the nearest chair, keeping his weapon in hand.

Unsure how to respond, Delcin moved behind his desk. "What are you proposing?"

"I propose we figure out a way to get us the hell off this station."

Delcin's thoughts still swirled out of control. He hadn't come to grips with what he'd seen in the control room yet. He was certainly not ready for round two with the *Doubtful* crew. "The alien will come around. He needs the sanction of a powerful ally to succeed. Your father and his little gang of thugs is not his solution. If I understand the situation correctly, the Consortium is likely the group that sabotaged his project in the first place. That leaves the Agency. He'll come around."

Once he'd said it, Delcin felt more like he believed it. Despite the alien's callous murder of the guards, ultimately he'd need Delcin and what Delcin stood for. *All I have to do is stand fast.* It was the damned *Doubtful* people. They'd drive anyone mad.

Rogers shrugged. "All right. You can be delusional if you want. I'm trying to come up with practical solutions." He hesitated as if considering a bit of conversation, then leaned forward, looking at him intently across the desk. "Did you notice the alien is losing energy?"

"Losing energy? What do you mean?"

"The longer this standoff goes on, the alien is having a harder time manifesting himself. We noticed, after that little temper tantrum it just had, that it vanished altogether. That could mean it's unable to sustain its form as Jak Moster."

"What other form would it come in?"

"The one that came to our ship last year was more like a glowing ball of light than a human. It spoke to each person in his or her own language and appeared at least to the mind's eye as someone significant to the individual."

Delcin studied the young man. He seemed sincere. Delcin was at a disadvantage because he'd never dealt with the Ancients before this encounter. Every time he'd spoken with this particular alien, he'd appeared as Jak. He had nothing to compare it with.

Or maybe Rogers thinks you're a stupid ass and he can get you to believe anything.

"So what do you propose? That we reboot it? Plug it in?"

Rogers' brow furrowed. "No. I propose that we use the alien's weakness to get the hells off this station, before it kills the rest of us!"

Delcin snorted with derision. "Perhaps you need to worry about that. Certainly I don't need to. The Ancient needs me to provide him with services and a market for his technology."

The other man stared at him. "Are you serious? You really think it differentiates you from us in the scheme of things? Come on,

Delcin." He started for the door. "We're all as expendable as a spanner or a prototool."

Nonsense. There had to be a way to get this station going. Tuon Donn wouldn't allow any other outcome. The mission meant he had to stay here, and in charge, until that happened. He conveniently shoved aside the memory, and the smell, of his officers frying under the alien's charge of lightning.

"I don't believe you."

"Delcin, what in the name of the heavens do I have to lose right now, that I would lie to you? The end is coming, and it's coming fast. I'm asking you to stand with us if we hit a crisis. All of us together may be able to take the alien down. At least long enough to get to safety."

He didn't want to hear any more of this. He had to distract Rogers, before his words made Delcin think too much. He had orders, damn it. He couldn't challenge them. Not if he wanted to succeed.

"You know, your father intends to make a trade for you, anyway. So next time they're in range of the station, we'll likely be sending you back. All this drama really isn't necessary."

The other man frowned. "A trade for what?"

Delcin smirked. "We're about to acquire some Bellonan breeding stock."

Rogers eyed him a long moment, and the uncertainty in his eyes showed his calculations. Finally, he tucked his weapon in his belt. And laughed.

"Whoa, you really have been duped by this whole system. Did my father actually say that? Because I'm pretty sure he'd never do anything of the sort. He values each member of his crew as if they were his own child. The Bellonans are no different."

But it had seemed like such a sure thing! Which of them was lying?

"We'll see, now, won't we?"

Rogers waved a hand, dismissing him. "Fine. You stay holed up in your office here all alone and wait for the end. Because we're going to bring this fiasco to a close, one way or another. You can have your station. Hope it brings you all the glory and profit you want."

Breathing hard, red-faced, Rogers left the room, slamming the door behind him.

Delcin's hands started to tremble, and he grabbed the edge of the desk to still them. He wasn't going to fall apart, not now. He had a deal with this alien. He'd capture the station and transfer its ownership to the Agency. He just had to think. He was an amazing puzzle solver. He'd just take some time and work out the situation's new parameters.

He took a seat at his desk, and reached into the drawer for his flask. It was half full. Good. That should just about fuel the rest of his musings. Tommy Rogers may think he had a handle on their situation, but he was wrong. Maybe even dead wrong.

CHAPTER 21

TEMMS stood once again on Lennor, on the grassy plain in front of the Lenci's caves. The thin priests' multi-colored robes blew in the slight breeze. The air smelled of wildflowers and fresh cut fields.

"Greetings," he called to the priests, who stood perhaps thirty meters away, three large cloth-covered baskets at their feet. "Our thanks for allowing us to come to your world."

"They don't look happy," said Nikki, who'd joined them from Garrett Rawls' crew. Her blonde hair was pulled back into a ponytail, and she wore heavy leather vest and chaps over her clothing.

"No, they don't," Riviera agreed.

The tallest one of the bald men eyed them with suspicion. "I trust you do not believe you may continue to come here and pillage our culture's artifacts indefinitely."

"Not at all," Temms replied. "This is an emergency, as I said when we hailed you. A danger to the entire system."

"So you said." The priests just stared at him, the short one waving his urn of incense on a long stick. "I have conferred with my companions, and we agree that in addition to the payment, that you, yourself, accompany the team below to prove your commitment to the cause."

The wind changed and the *Doubtful* team got a faceful of the sharp, reeking incense.

"Horrid stink, that is," Riviera grumbled. "Hoped I never have to smell it again in my life."

"Not too late to un-volunteer," Temms said. "I can take D with us. I'd rather take you, because you've been there already."

The large, dark-skinned woman eyed the priests, who seemed quite unwelcoming. "That I have. Which is why I tell you again, it ain't a good idea for you to go down in the caves. The priestess said—"

He leaned close, speaking quietly. "I know what the priestess said, that the men don't come back. I also remember she said that they don't tell the men the safe way out of the caves to keep hold of the ruling power in the tribes, too. Under the circumstances, I think you know how to get out." He looked her in the eye. "You do, right?"

She nodded, bottom lip sticking out in a pout. "Don't make me feel no better about the prospects, Captain."

He contained a growl that insinuated itself through his frustrated chest. He turned to Dani, who waited, armed, just behind Riviera and Nikki. Their slipcraft shone in reflected sunlight behind them. "The mission should be straightforward, if the Lumina's records are correct. We're in, then out, with the part we seek."

Dani's skin beaded up with sweat in the full sun. "You're sure these priests are being honest, right?"

Temms studied the priests. "They didn't give us a problem last time. Just keep an eye on them. If Riviera or I call you, then come into the caves and see what's gone wrong."

"Yes, sir," Dani said.

"Come on. Let's meet the home team."

Temms led the small party to where the Lenci stood, putting a smile on his face and keeping it there. The chief priest, Malka, scowled as they approached. His hairless legs stuck out from underneath his blue robe, his feet bare in the worn grass. He waved a bony finger in Temms' direction.

"No good will come of this!" he cried. "Your women hardly escaped the last time you came. The Kiritan is mighty!"

The priests chanted "Ommmm, ommmm," as Malka spoke, and the little one with the incense hurried around the group like a possessed dervish, smoke trailing after him.

Temms spoke slowly, trying to match the cadence in his voice to that of the priest, hoping it would win him over. "We are aware of the Kiritan, father. As you say, my people have felt its claws and teeth. But our need is great. The Ancients hold hostage our crew, and demand this sacrifice. So come we must."

He set down the box of trinkets and tools he'd promised as payment. "As we agreed."

"You dare enter the caves yourself?" Malka asked, trembling where he stood.

He must have thought I'd change my mind instead. Guess he doesn't know me very well.

"I must," Temms replied. "I cannot ask my people to go where I am afraid to walk."

Besides, if I'd stayed on the damned station instead of leaving my people there alone, we might not be in this mess. Whatever's going to happen here, it's going to happen with me front and center.

Malka shuddered. The expression in the old priest's eye was one of absolute terror. "You will die."

"Let's hope not, shall we?" He cleared his throat, the priest's fretfulness starting to get to him. "Riviera? Nikki?"

"When you be ready, sir." Riviera exchanged glances with Dani. "If we call, you'd best be comin', blasting full tilt."

"Gotcha." Dani winked. "We'll hold the ground here, sir. Don't you worry." She took a position between the priests and the cave.

"Not you I'm worried about, D."

"This just gets better and better," Nikki muttered. "Next flip of the coin, I'm cheating so Val has to come."

The captain nodded to the women. Each picked up a basket stuffed with incense sticks and pieces of bone and meat to distract the Kiritan. When he'd taken one last breath of the air above ground, he headed into the cave, Nikki and Riviera on his heels.

It didn't take long from the cave entrance to feel the dank, wet air sink into his bones. He clicked on his flashlight, shining it from one side of the brown clay tunnel to the other. The color faded into grayness as he tried to see farther ahead. The fine mist grew colder and took on a sulfurous smell.

"Ugh," he said, the sound of his boots echoing against the cave walls. "That incense would actually be an improvement."

"Good thing," Riviera muttered. "'Cause this is just about where we start needing it."

"Tell me again about the incense?" Nikki asked.

Riviera fumbled in her pocket for an ignition source. "For some reason, this stench sends the Kiritan away. Think with the three of us having some, we should be fine 'til we get back outside." When she found it, she lit the end of the incense. The brief blaze-up revealed two corridors, one forking off to the left, the other proceeding straight ahead. An eerie howl came from the one straight ahead.

Nikki shivered. "That's horrible."

"That them?" Temms asked.

"Sure is, sir. We best watch ourselves now." Riviera stopped, listening. "Oh, and there be a hole in the floor real soon coming up." Her sheepish grin reflected bright in the flashlight beam. "The one I fell into last time. No sense in risking a broken leg with the shortcut, if we don't have to."

"Absolutely agree." He swept the floor with the beam, trying to locate the drop. The howl sounded again along the corridor ahead. Closer this time.

"So do we just leave this food?" Nikki asked, poking through the contents of the basket. "I don't think we've got time for a barbecue."

"Yes. Women say it's treated with some kind of drug that delay the Kiritan's reaction. Hope it's long enough to do what we need to do." Riviera shifted the basket into her other hand so she could carry her incense, burning, in front of her.

Temms swept the open space before them with his scanner. He got mostly static, but the device detected something in the depths below them. They'd have to get closer. "Riviera, last time you were here, you said there were two?"

"Three. We kept them controlled with these hunks of meat and the burning sticks."

"So just three?"

Riviera shrugged. "We didn't get so far into the cave. For all I know, there could be a whole nest of 'em back there by now."

"Wonderful." Nikki toyed with the incense. When another howl came from the corridors ahead of them, she finally lit one. "They're flesh-eating beasts, right? That's what the report said."

Temms nodded.

"And what's the deal with men? They don't like men?"

Riviera grinned. "Guess it's the women's way of keeping some power on their side. They be priestesses and don't tell the men about their secret tunnels. When men come down, guess they don't come back."

Nikki eyed Temms. "Then you're an idiot."

Like I need more people reminding me that.

"Whatever." He studied his scanner. The life sign signatures were definitely clearer this time, but they were on the distant edges of the scan. "I'm picking up several beasts, but none are in our vicinity at this point. Maybe we'll miss them."

The air, devoid of wind or movement, felt heavy, crushing, its thick smell filling his lungs with putrid glory. Whatever was in the baskets stank as well. He reached into the basket Riviera carried and hauled out a large bone with meat on it, tossing it over to the corridor from which the howl had come. "Which way to the coordinates the Lumina gave us?"

She studied her scanner. "Look like it's down this corridor." She gestured to the left.

"All right, I'll fire up that incense stick, too. Drop some more of those bones. We'd be better off having these things busy up here while we're scouting below. We need to get in and out."

Trailing aromatic smoke, the three of them marched down the left corridor, watching all around for traces of the beasts. Several piles of gnawed bones marked the turns in the hallways they passed, left over from other travelers who'd come this way. Other howls echoed in the distance. Their eerie pitch gave him the heebie-jeebies. Nikki twitched every time the sound came. A glance at Riviera showed her usual stony expression. He couldn't tell whether she was disarmed by the beasts or not.

I'm supposed to be the one setting the leadership example here. Pull it together.

For an added measure of courage, he tucked the basket into the crook of his left arm and took out his pistol. He remembered from Liang's report that the two of them had been able to use a lasergun to hold off an attack by the Kiritan. Hold off, but not kill. They must be powerful beasts indeed.

"What do they look like again?" he asked.

"About so big," Riviera replied, holding a hand waist-high. "Wiry gray fur, thick body like a herdbeast. Stinks like a wet dog. Claws long as my fingers. Strong body that can stand right up on its back legs. But the eyes—" She shuddered. "They be bright blue, like a laser light. Seems like they'd burn right through you."

"Got it. With any luck, we won't see one."

"Here's hoping, sir."

Nikki took a step back, visually checking the route behind them. Riviera checked her scanner again, directing them to take another left into an enclosed path where the short ceiling made them bend over to continue. Water had condensed on the walls here, draining down onto the clay floor, making it slippery. Footing was treacherous, even more so when the ceiling opened up into a large cave, but the path took a sudden downward turn.

With nothing to hold onto other than the slimy walls or each other, they had slow going to reach the bottom of the cave floor, along a drop that had to be one hundred meters or more. Nikki dropped her char twice and had to slip through the spongy clay to retrieve it, sliding all the way to the bottom of the path. Temms lurched through a particularly soft spot and tumbled over a lump in the path, dropping his basket. He retrieved it as fast as he could, keeping the bones in the basket so as not to call any of the creatures. After some final bumps and bruises, they arrived at the lower level.

"Best I can tell, the parts we looking for are in another chamber like the one Liang found up above," Riviera said. "Seem to be set at regular intervals apart, like they've been catalogued." She consulted her equipment again. "Up ahead on the right."

"Good."

"You stay back, Captain," Nikki said. "Let the women go first." He started to protest, but the slight blonde shut him down. "You're the one who pointed out the danger to men. We'll handle it."

Temms reluctantly let them lead the way along the path into the series of chambers, which they reached without further mishap. "Keep your scanner tuned for Kiritan. We want to know they're coming before they get here."

"Yes, sir."

Riviera took position as guard at the only entry to the round chamber, while Nikki and Temms went inside. A quick flip of Temms' flashlight showed a number of bricked-in slots ranged along the walls. He set down his basket and lasergun, then cocked his head, listening to the sound of water slowly dripping into a puddle. The dull hollowness of its sound indicated to him that they were quite deep in the cave. A long way between them and the outside, particularly if they encountered the Kiritan.

"So where are these artifacts?" Nikki asked. "Behind those bricks?" She frowned and picked at one. "How do they open? Magic words or something?"

"Nothing that easy," he said. He called up Liang's report on his scanning device, double-checking how she'd been able to open the portals when she'd come to the caverns. "Liang had to break through the walls into a small space protected by a clear field."

"Oh, so you've done this before." Nikki's voice lost some of its tightness, sounding almost relieved.

"Some of us have."

He knocked the bricks clear on several of the containers, then set his lasergun at the frequency of the transparency that still protected the artifacts. The one piece of the *odahmeen* he needed was roughly the size of a shoebox, with two odd shaped extensions on one side. He walked along the space he'd opened, and identified the one he sought almost immediately. His gaze was captured by the coppery sheen of the other bits tucked away in their protected slots. Should he take them all? Who knew to what use he could put them in the days to come? He could have his team construct any number of useful items if he just had the right ones.

No.

He'd had enough of the Ancients and their mysteries and their powers. Once he got his people from the station, he intended to steer clear of them and their artifacts once and for all.

He'd just opened the slot he wanted when Riviera gasped.

"Captain? Best hurry. Got three on the way!"

"Nik, light another one of those damned sticks." He fumbled with the bulky artifact, wrestling it into his backpack. Taking one last, longing look at the shiny artifacts, he tore himself away. "Let's go."

They hurried out of the cul-de-sac, heading for the path back to the surface. Too late Temms realized that they'd have to climb the steep path that had been precarious enough on the way down. Making it up that slick clay, especially with the spots they'd torn into the passageway, would be a nightmare. They made several abortive attempts, then surrendered to the reality. An alternate path led under the hill.

"Which way are the monsters coming?" he asked.

A roar sounded from their right, and he turned just in time to spot one of the creatures coming from behind the hill. Another roar rumbled from overhead, one at the top of the hill. Looks like it was the path ahead. "Go on!" he yelled. He handed Riviera the laden backpack and shoved her in the direction of the opening that led under the hill.

Moments later, a deep growl came from the exact hole he'd been planning to escape through, followed by a huge gray blur galloping in their direction. Riviera, in front of him, skidded to a stop. He grabbed her arm, but he couldn't move the large woman. Instead, he used his momentum to propel himself in front of her.

"Here!" Nikki yelled. But it wasn't the little blonde's coquettish voice at all. It was a deeper, male voice. The blur continued past Temms and Riviera, going for the man that now stood just beyond them. Nicholas, the gender alter ego of Nikki. She/he was drawing the animal away from them. It landed just in front of Nik, issuing a haunting howl.

"Go on!" Nik called. "Get the parts safely away!"

Torn for just a moment, Temms got his feet under him and sent Riviera on. "Get that back to the ship," he ordered. When she cleared his field of vision, he swiveled to face the beast again. "Nik, you need to go on, too. Garrett won't forgive me if I get you killed down here."

The beast hesitated, hearing the second voice behind it. It swung its big head in Temms' direction, sniffing, and growled. The blue eyes seemed to pierce him, just like laserfire. They even sounded like—no, that was Riviera shooting from behind him. So close that he was temporarily blinded by the light. He tried to stumble aside, hoping the Kiritan was blinded as well.

Nik took the opportunity to move, too, keeping himself on the opposite side of the animal from the captain. "You're the one with a mission, Captain. You need to get that part up above to complete your device, get your people back. I've got some skills you haven't seen yet. I can avoid this monster."

Temms studied the young man across the shoulder of the stinking beast. "Yeah, but this isn't the only one we've got to avoid. Get over on this side and I'll cover you while we head up."

Nicholas grimaced in a way very reminiscent of his alter ego. "Chivalry doesn't serve you here, Captain. I promise. Please go."

Did the gender-shifting alien really have some magic at hand to escape? Temms had seen stranger things. "All right," he conceded. He backed away from the Kiritan, following the direction he'd sent Riviera. Footsteps behind him revealed that she actually hadn't left at all, despite his direct command. *Did everyone intend to be stupid?*

"Don't my orders mean anything?" he roared at her.

The sudden yell grabbed the attention of the beast, and it turned to face him, crouching before it leapt straight at him.

The solid heavy weight of the animal hit him like a moving wall, knocking him flat on his back. Paws landed on his stomach, and claws sliced into his skin. He couldn't breathe. As he struggled to move, the animal looked down at him and its jaws opened slowly. Teeth as long as his thumb lined that terrible mouth, pointy, sharp and white. Saliva dripped down onto his face. The beast's breath smelled like rotting meat.

Temms gagged, trying to roll out from under the thing, but its weight pinned him to the clay, which oozed up around his bare neck. He heard more growls, and more laserfire, but it was in a different direction, no flash. Riviera yelled something unintelligible, then keyed the communit, calling Dani's name. Nicholas/Nikki stabbed at the beast with a sharp blade that flashed in the half-light, but it ignored him, intent on its fallen prey.

The Kiritan sniffed at him curiously, then opened its mouth wide and buried its teeth in his shoulder. Once it had a good bite, it yanked its head sideways, tearing more than flesh. He got his fist up and punched the animal in the snout, but it was too late. The terrible pain of the attack overwhelmed him, and he lost consciousness.

CHAPTER 22

IN the control room, Benzi studied the scheme he'd drawn out on his data pad, not wanting the Ancient to see his scribblings. It was almost time. He leaned close to Uri, who was sitting next to him, looking busy.

"You up for this, boy? Hate to see you get zapped again."

Uri eyed him, jaw set. "It is my duty. I am always capable."

"Good boy." Benzi grinned, hardly noticing that Uri wasn't human. Since they'd been trapped on the station, such things had taken on much less importance. Survival was what counted.

He glanced over to Tommy, who lounged carelessly in his chair. The Ancient stood at his usual spot, and he, too, had noticed Tommy's lack of attention to the assigned task of finding the missing parts. His gaze returned repeatedly to the captain's son, and his fingers trembled as he worked his keyboard. But his form remained solid.

Benzi next turned to Liang, who tapped away on her keys, and Iov, who stood just outside the door, watching for the sign. They were ready.

Nim sat at the most distant terminal, following some protocol Liang had set. Benzi wasn't too sure about the man, not yet. He'd turned on them once. Sure, Liang had explained the whole chip thing, but Benzi had been burnt many times by too-easy trust. Better to stick to what you knew for sure.

"Here's hoping," Benzi muttered under his breath. He nodded to Iov.

The Muuvo came running into the control room, stopping at Liang's station. "The food's gone! What am I supposed to feed my brother and me, hmm?" He slammed a thick hand on the edge of her monitor, knocking it sideways. It flew off her desk and hit the floor with a loud crack.

Liang jumped to her feet. "What have you done?"

Benzi snuck a peek at the Ancient, who positively quivered with irritation. So far, so good. "You ready?" he whispered to Uri.

Uri nodded, eyes wide.

Tommy put his feet up on his desk and laughed. "C'mon, you guys. What's the problem?"

Iov crossed his arms, feet shoulder-width apart. "I can't guarantee any sort of quality work under these circumstances. Now that the Agency's been cut off, the food's run out. I demand you do something about it immediately."

Liang nodded slowly. "You're right, Iov." She turned to the Ancient. "What are we going to do about food supplies?"

Tommy cackled. "Here's that chance to lose five pounds you were always blabbing about back on the ship."

Unexpectedly, Nim got up, shoving his chair into the wall. "You shut up about her! You don't have the right to criticize her!"

Startled, Benzi blinked. This wasn't part of the script. *Oh, well. Guess we go with it.* "Okay, kid. Go."

Uri made himself as small as possible and crawled along the backs of the consoles, on the far side from the Ancient. The argument among the others got louder, Liang and Iov continuing to harangue the Ancient about food and supplies, while Nim walked over and shoved Tommy in his chair, knocking it to the ground.

"Stop this! Stop at once." The Ancient tried to be heard over the commotion, but the team ignored him. "Stop!"

Tommy pulled himself up off the ground and took a swing at Nim, catching him on the chin. Nim roared and punched Tommy in the gut.

Hunkered down behind his screen, Benzi split his attention among the participants. The Ancient had definitely been affected by the lack of control, his face flushed and body vibrating. Uri continued to make his way to the back of the Ancient's console. Everything was going as they'd hoped. *So far.*

Once Nim was hit, Liang threw herself into the free-for-all, screaming in an emotional release that Benzi hadn't believed the reserved first officer capable of. Nim pulled her off Tommy, still swinging. Iov moved away from them, destroying another monitor as he demanded appropriate food. Tommy backed away, too, triangulating the Ancient's attention.

"Stop!" the Ancient shouted, and he let loose an electrical bolt that missed Tommy by inches, scarring the wall.

Damn me, that happened sooner than I expected. Benzi surreptitiously checked for Uri's location. The young Muuvo was crouched next to the Ancient's console, tools in hand, frantically digging at the power source.

We need more time.

Benzi got up and walked over to Iov, shoving his shoulder. "What in Sprechan's name are you doing, man? Who's gonna pay for the repair of this equipment, hmm?"

"I'm not paying for anything. I don't even want to be here. And I'm finished helping this alien punish us all."

Iov marched out the door.

"Come back here!" the Ancient shouted, and electricity crackled all around him. He vanished for a moment, then returned.

Yes! It was working! Have to ratchet up the tension.

"You know, he's right," Benzi called, challenging the Ancient. "Why should we help you? You're gonna kill us now, or later—"

"Quinn, don't!" Liang's face showed genuine concern.

Right, it might be stupid. But Uri's part in this was crucial. He needed time to finish. "Or what are you going to do about it, Liang? Want to spank me?" He leered at her, fighting the laugh that bubbled inside him at the expressions of Nim and Tommy at his words.

"She's your superior officer, you ass. You follow her orders," Tommy barked.

"Make me."

He cocked an eyebrow at the captain's son, hands out in a "come-and-get-me" beckon.

Tommy ran toward him, ready to do violence. Before he reached him, though, the Ancient shot off another bolt that knocked Tommy right into Benzi, and they both fell to the ground.

A second later, he heard a loud pop and a diminishing of the mechanical hum that normally filled the deck. The Ancient squawked with rage and then he was gone.

"Quinn?"

"Rogers?"

Liang and Nim spoke almost simultaneously, hurrying over to help the two up. Tommy had a nasty burn across his shoulder, but Benzi was unharmed, other than a sore back.

"Thanks for being my shield, pal." He grinned at Tommy, secretly proud to have the captain's pride and joy take one to save Benzi's skin.

"Yeah, no problem," Tommy growled.

They all turned to the Ancient's station, where their tormentor remained notably absent.

"Uri?" Benzi called.

No answer.

He threaded his way through the consoles, finding the young Muuvo unconscious on the floor next to the Ancient's terminal. He was still breathing. "Hey, I need help here! Someone get Iov."

Nim came running, and he and Benzi moved Uri to the rest space the Ancient had let them build on the far side of the room so they wouldn't have to take time from their work. Iov returned, and he sat with Uri, communing in some odd ritual, until he woke up.

Liang tended to Tommy's burn with some ointment and a bandage. "You think it's gone?" she asked, with a gesture at the Ancient's space.

"He's been weakening every day. If our theory was right, he draws on the station power to manifest. My best guess is, since Uri managed to short out the juice to his console, he'll take a hit."

Nim frowned. "But when it figures out what we did—"

Benzi nodded. "You guessed it. The rest of us will be toast, too."

CHAPTER 23

BEEP. Beep. Beep.

Noise penetrated Temms' fogged mind, but he couldn't open his eyes. Voices. Women talking. He couldn't make out what they were saying.

A moment later, he was back on Gilada, hearing women talking at Tommy's ball game. Mothers, sitting all around him, comparing their offspring's various abilities. *How's Tommy playing?* he wanted to say. *Is he safe? Is he home safe?*

He couldn't speak.

Beep.

Something was wrong. That much he knew. Searching for his last memory, all he could grasp was a cloudy sense of panic, fear and loathing. But he couldn't place himself anywhere.

What was I doing?

Why couldn't he wake up? That seemed more disturbing than anything else. He was barely there. He felt no pain. So whatever had happened must have just been a shock to his system. He'd wake up soon.

He had to.

Maybe he could get a clue from what the women were saying. He tried very hard to focus on that conversation.

A young, distressed voice. "Has he responded yet?"

"No, love." This alto voice sounded weary but reassuring. "He'll take his time. When he's ready to rejoin us, he will."

The other woman again. "I shouldn't have—there were things I should have said to him. I've got to get a chance to apologize." A silence. "I know he's moved on now. Maybe he needs someone else who's a captain—"

The second woman burst out laughing. "Oh, honey, no. Perhaps that's been your error all along. Being a captain would absolutely doom any chance of things becoming serious between them. A captain isn't at liberty to love anyone on his or her crew. They are like those of the religious orders. They've married a higher power, the lure of a ship and the stars." Another silence. "But Temms seems like a man who is straightforward. He must have told you this."

Sniffling. "He did. I thought—I don't know. I thought he was just putting me off, that I'd done something wrong, or he was being petty or—" More sniffling and a blown nose. "He's been so very kind to me, and we'd been close. I was sure that eventually he and—I would...."

Someone touched his hand. He realized with a start that feeling was returning to his body.

The second woman spoke in a confidential tone. "My dear doctor, as devoted as you have been in the last five days, I can easily see that you care a great deal for Temms Rogers. Believe me when I say that if he could give his heart to anyone, I'm sure it would be you."

Are they talking about me? Who am I supposed to be in love with? What's going on?

Another voice, male. "Come on, Val. Let's let him rest, and let the doctor tend her patients."

"A moment, C.T." A whisper close to his ear. "You come back to us soon, Temms. Your work is not completed, my dear."

Movement in the room. Then the noise settled. *Beep. Beep. Beep.* The rhythmic repetition lulled him, and he lost himself again.

* * *

CAPTAIN Rogers?

Temms struggled to pay attention. The darkness was warm and welcoming around him. He could remain here, safe and comfortable, forever. Why did people keep calling him?

Captain Rogers, please. We need you.

WHO IS THIS?

It's Monty, sir. Can you hear me?

I—I CAN. I THOUGHT YOU WERE ON THE PLANET.

I was with the Lumina—my sister—yes. The boy's mental voice changed when he said "sister". A delight filled his tone. *Captain Dutton retrieved me and brought me back to the ship to see if I could help.*

Temms couldn't open his eyes, though he tried. *WHERE AM I?*

In the infirmary, sir. You've been here nearly a week. Do you remember the caves of Lennor? The Kiritan?

Visions that had plagued his sleep poked at his consciousness, dreams of sharp teeth and claws, of blood and violence. He let them slip away again, because they were disturbing.

Captain, it's important that you listen to me. The doctor says there may not be much time.

MUCH TIME FOR—WHAT ARE YOU TALKING ABOUT? Confusion set in. Temms wanted to retreat into that dark, comfortable place, but Monty's mental voice was insistent. *HOW CAN I UNDERSTAND YOU?*

I have learned much from my sister. I can maintain a mental contact with people who relate to me.

The strain of trying to sort through even these simple facts wore him out. *I'M SO TIRED. PLEASE LET ME REST.*

I wish I could, Captain. We need your knowledge of the artifacts now, before…in case….

The boy's thoughts seemed to stumble for the first time. What was it he was trying to say? Temms considered the words, but couldn't put his finger on the message.

Please. Captain. We need you. My father needs you. He's still trapped on the station. Please help us.

Station? On the station. A flash of an invisible door, Benzi. Liang. Tommy. Jak Moster. And Delcin. A flush of heat ran through him. They had his crew. The darkness receded and the light grew around him.

Good. Good. You aren't able to get up. The doctor can explain it to you when we've finished. But if you're awake, I can maintain this link even down in engineering. Dani gave me the schematics Father sent. We can construct this object.

YOU CAN'T GIVE IT TO THEM. EVEN IF IT WOULD SAVE OUR PEOPLE. THEY'LL DESTROY EVERYTHING.

I know. My sister has shown me the texts. We studied them together. We may be able to use the device to gain access to the station while keeping full control of it. That's all we have to do, in order to rescue them. Please hold on, at least that long. Think of Jak, and of Agent Delcin. That will help you focus. Listen for my mind.

I'LL TRY, MONTY. I'LL TRY.

The boy kept up a monologue all the way to his father's workstation, nothing important, details about his visit with his sister, the upcoming ceremony. Every time Temms would feel himself drifting off, Monty apparently sensed it, because he'd drop a hint about Tommy or the Agency, something designed to remind Temms of his anger. Must have worked, too. He stayed with Monty, pace for pace.

I'm in engineering now, Captain. I have the three parts spread out here on the table. Can you see them?

Temms' first instinct was to snap that of course he couldn't see them. He couldn't even open his eyes. But he found that he had a shadowy vision of the table and the objects on it. *AM I SEEING THROUGH YOUR EYES? YOUR SISTER HAS SHARED MANY GIFTS.*

I hoped that would happen. Good. Let's begin.

Temms was no engineer, but he'd been aboard the station and in contact with the Ancient posing as Jak Moster. Monty was a savant who had no direct knowledge of the *odahmeen*. With the two of them working together, the artifacts were gradually assembled into a single device. With the final snap, the *odahmeen* hummed to life. No lights blinked, nothing changed on the exterior, but Temms could feel the energy pulsing through Monty's fingers.

WHAT NOW?

A burst of white light filled Temms' consciousness, and he nearly lost the connection with Monty.

WHAT'S HAPPENING? SOMEONE PLEASE EXPLAIN.

A neutral voice filled his head, not male, not female, not Monty.

Temms Rogers, the activation of the device has alerted us to the state of matters. You have been sorely used by one of our kind, and I must apologize. This being has used his powers for evil, and in the process, innocents have been injured or killed.

KILLED? IS TOMMY DEAD? LIANG? THE OF MY CREW?

Thoughts came too fast now, and the light came too close. Pain filled his body and his consciousness. The darkness was far away and he thought to plunge into it once again, to escape from the anguish of life.

They live, Captain, and they will return to you. The odahmeen can open the station hatch, though it cannot allow you to board the station. Your people can be rescued, if you have a way to cross the space between your ship and the hatch.

His mind went into problem-solving mode. *CAN WE SEND A SLIPCRAFT? NO, IT COULD BE DESTROYED BEFORE IT ARRIVES. THE—THE TUNNEL! IF WE CAN GET CLOSE ENOUGH....*

Very good, Captain.

I'll tell Dani, sir. She'll get that activated.

Fighting the pain, Temms found his eyes suddenly open. Okalani stood over him, mouth open, tears in her eyes. She gasped and jumped back when he surfaced, falling into Garrett's unsuspecting arms. Temms moaned, the pain threatening to take over his thoughts.

"Let me give you something for that, Temms," the doctor said, pulling herself together, scrambling to deal with his state. "We'd held you in a forced coma to let your body heal. Hoping it would, anyway."

She injected him with something, and within a few minutes, the pain receded to a nearly manageable level.

Temms tried to focus on Garrett. What was he doing here? He couldn't make the words come out.

"Hey, there, friend," Garrett said. "Don't worry your head about a dang thing. We've all taken turns over here making sure your crew has everything they need. You just get yourself well again, you hear me?"

Temms studied the *Six-Shooter's* captain, seeing weary lines in his face and worry in his eyes. Everyone who stood around the bed wore the same look. Monty had said there was an issue of it being "too late." Had he meant Temms wasn't expected to recover? These expressions certainly seemed to bear that out.

THEN I'M GOING TO GO DOWN FIGHTING.

Temms reached back inside, seeking the third voice again.

WHO ARE YOU?

I am of the race you call Ancients, brought here by the activation of a device we thought long dead. A scan of your records has educated us on the current situation. This is exactly the scenario we sought to avoid when we struck a deal with the Consortium many centuries ago. Those of our kind without our self-imposed moral compunctions have always tried to take advantage of those we call our children. For this reason only, we may allow the odahmeen to be used one last time. Then it must be destroyed.

Temms sensed movement. It took a few moments to realize he wasn't the one who was moving, but Monty, carrying a part of his consciousness along with him down to the port where the tunnel was to be used. The sensation disoriented him, and he found it difficult to concentrate.

"Temms?" Okalani stood on his right side, and she took his hand. Her fingers were warm on his. He forced his lips to move. They felt like useless flaps of flesh. He couldn't make them form conversation. She wiped away a quick tear.

"Honey, please don't strain yourself. We have waited so long for just a sign that you'd come back to us." She sniffled. "Is your pain level all right? Can I give you something else? Get you anything?"

He managed to shake his head slightly. The movement felt odd. He sensed that parts of his body were immobilized, wrapped tight somehow. Not every part of his body seemed under his control. His right hand, the one Okalani held, felt most normal of all. He was glad she was speaking to him again, and not mad any more.

They're activating the device now! Look, the station door is opening!

Monty's sheer joy at the success of his experiment washed over Temms, bringing him some comfort. Maybe this whole ordeal was nearly over. He held onto that faint mental voice for dear life, knowing the next few minutes would mean the difference for his hostage crew between life and death.

CHAPTER 24

WHEN the Ancient returned it didn't exact punishment at all.

It apologized for the food situation, and promised to get new supplies. "Please, let's get back to work," it said. "There isn't much time."

Liang eyed the alien suspiciously. "What about the equipment?" she asked.

"We have replacements on the lower deck. Get them installed."

Sure enough, the damaged monitors were much too easily replaced. The Ancient's console never recovered power—at least they'd accomplished that much—but it just moved to another station.

By that evening, she completed her sweep of Perpetra with a weary sigh and stabbed a finger at her keyboard, sending the information to the monitor where the Ancient waited, looking pale and faint. "Not there," she said.

"Then we begin on Marriel."

Liang's heart sank. Had they really gone through all of that for nothing? She wanted to protest that the day had gone on much too long, since the alien's earlier outburst and the murder of the Agency guards. Would it matter?

She formulated a complaint, but never got to lodge it.

The alien suddenly jerked upright. "No, they can't!" His outline vibrated, his manifestation pushed to the max. "It's mine! I've won it. I must be allowed to finish!"

"Can't what?" she asked, confused. But it didn't seem to be speaking to her.

At the same time, Benzi jumped, reaching for his back pocket. "It's my communit," he hissed.

Tommy reached for his. "Mine too." He hastily read a text message. "The *Doubtful's* got the shield down. It's time. We've got to go, now!"

The Ancient had first gone pale, but now was red with fury. Liang glanced around and counted all the *Doubtful* people. No better time than while they were all together. She frantically gathered her datapad and small equipment. Iov grabbed Uri and shoved him toward the door. Benzi tossed all his disks into his pack and bailed for the exit, too. Nim and Tommy took a stance blocking the way to the door from the alien's potential sizzle and flame, waiting for Liang to pass before they, too, left.

"Why didn't he attack us?" Liang asked Tommy as they ran.

"Beats me. He looked mad enough to explode."

"How much time do we have?" Iov asked.

Benzi read the message aloud. "Have assistance of Ancient aboard for rescue. Report to the landing deck hatch immediately."

"The message was from Dani Jamar," Tommy mused. "Why isn't it from my father?"

"Maybe we ain't a priority for him if he's got another of these bastards on the ship with him," Benzi growled.

Liang headed off a retort. "What about Delcin and the doctor? And the others?"

"What about them?" Tommy didn't slow his run.

The lights flickered overhead and went dark for a moment, before coming back on at half strength. "What's that about then?" Benzi asked, looking around suspiciously.

An angry roar echoed through the corridors of the station, followed by the sharp snap of electric bolts. "You can't do this to me!"

"No time to find out. Move it!" Tommy yelled.

The group skittered into the landing bay and ran for the hatch. The protective layer of air that held atmosphere inside the station was active. Liang identified half a dozen of the mercenary captain's group ships in the air outside the station, as well as the *Doubtful*. Delcin's *Shelim* wasn't in sight. That seemed significant.

The station suddenly shook, knocking them from their feet. The alien's angry voice again echoed through the halls and bays.

"This is my territory now, not yours. You have no right to interfere. I will bring control and prosperity to this system. It's mine."

"Who's he talking to?" Uri wanted to know.

"No idea. I don't think it's us. Or our ship. Maybe the Ancients are fighting with each other." Tommy frowned. "In which case it'll probably get messy, and you're right, I *should* get Delcin and the others."

Benzi snorted. "If Himself might get his head out of his arse long enough to listen."

"Hey, he gets one shot at this. After that, we're leaving."

Liang peered out the open hatch, seeing the *Doubtful* maneuvering into position to send the Tunnel across. "Hurry. We don't have much time. Who knows when this will stop?"

Tommy nodded. "You go, all of you, at first opportunity. That's an order. I'll go get the Agency people. Don't wait for me."

Liang was suddenly struck by how much Tommy sounded like his father. Even if she outranked him, that "order" resonated with her as if the captain had said it. The realization brought her a little smile.

"I'll come with you," Nim said. "There's four of them. They might need some convincing."

"I've got this," Liang assured them both. "Go."

They ran off. She watched anxiously as the *Doubtful* came close enough to send out the inflatable airlock.

Quinn stepped close and put his lips to her to ear. "What we gonna do about not having breathers, hmm? They're on the ship, not here. It's gonna be devilish cold. And how we gonna secure that lock to this hatch? Ain't no ratchets."

The idea of escape had come so abruptly, she hadn't puzzled out the details. A little thrill of fear and disappointment jolted through her. "I—I don't know. I guess that's your department." She turned to look into his eyes. "You're brilliant in improvise mode."

His eyes widened as he looked back at her. Finally he just laughed. "Right you are. Let me start thinking on that."

He pulled Iov aside, and the two of them started looking about the bay for something to use to fasten the lock. The entire exchange had been a civil one that the two of them could never have shared a year earlier. This experience had changed them. Liang was grateful for the transformation.

The lights flickered and went out, leaving the bay lit only by starlight from outside.

Uri stepped closer to her.

"Do you think we're going to really get out, Miss Liang?"

Words of vacant reassurance didn't easily come to her. She chose a more realistic tack. "This is our best chance. We just have to be ready to take it. Be brave. Think how the captain would act. He's waiting for us there, and he wants us to do the same."

The floor rumbled and shook under her feet. She lurched

sideways. "Let's just hope they hurry. Come on, we should find blankets or something to wrap up in to make that crossing. Extra clothing, jumpsuits, anything."

Her communit buzzed in the darkness.

"Liang, are you there?" purred Tasiq. "We're losing your readings."

"I'm here. The alien is having some sort of temper tantrum. I don't know how much longer we can remain safely."

"Dani's down at the lower hatch. The lock we have on the station is unstable, and we may lose it at any time. We don't have time to send over the usual equipment. We'll pressurize the tube as best we can from this end, and pump air and heat in, but we're not sure how long it will last. You may have to make a run for it."

"Understood. Mr. Quinn is prepared to secure the tube. Tommy's gone to roust up the remaining Agency people. Do we have permission to bring them aboard?"

"Stand by."

Seconds ticked past. Uri dropped a pile of heavy outerwear at her feet. "Found these," he said. He held up some clear face masks. "No oxygen, but they'll help keep in what we've got."

"Good. Get one on, and get some to Mr. Quinn and your brother, too."

She took the smallest coat, slipping it on over her shivering frame. Nerves were getting to her. How long before the Ancient appeared on the deck to electrocute them before they could escape?

Quinn shouted from the starboard side of the bay. "Got it, Liang. We can tie on here. It'll be rough, but we've got enough air inside the bay that we should be able to carry through if we don't lag about. "

Liang stared out at the stars. If this didn't work, the tube could slip, a rock plow through it, and they'd be left out floating among those little points of light forever. Imagining the cold, airless death that would follow shook her resolve. But she didn't show it. She had to set the example for young Uri and the others.

Tasiq came back on. "Captain Dutton says bring the Agency people. We'll have security waiting."

Captain Dutton? Why was he giving orders on the *Doubtful*? That anomaly shook her more than the idea of being stranded in space. What had happened to her captain?

"Understood. We're ready when you are."

The station shook again, hard this time. Several loose items crashed from shelves in the bay, and the noise made her jump. *We need to get off this station and soon.*

The lights came back on and the station stopped shaking. Simultaneously, the hatch on the *Doubtful* opened and the airlock tube appeared, telescoping outward in their direction.

Dani came on the comm. "Liang, Benzi, you've got to watch for this. Time's running out and we're going to have to just shoot it. We don't have a lot of control at your end, so get out of the way until it lands, then bail as fast as you can."

Liang acknowledged the warning. "It's coming!" she yelled over her shoulder.

She moved Uri to a safe spot out of reach of the swiftly-approaching end of the tube. It seemed to be on target for the hatch. She mentally rehearsed the steps they'd have to take next. Quinn and Iov would secure the tube, then they'd have to make a run through the padded interior to their own ship, praying that nothing went wrong. When Tommy and Nim reappeared, they'd bring the Agency people aboard. Then....

That's where the process broke down.

Normally, if they were attached to another ship, the crew of that vessel would detach the tube end once everyone was safely aboard, before the *Doubtful* retracted the airlock. They could hardly think the Ancient would blithely help them leave the station. So how would they release the end of the tube? Someone would have to do it manually.

That meant someone would have to ride the end of the tube without it being attached firmly to an anchor. The possibilities of how that could go wrong rushed through her imagination.

Some part of her that was still functioning in the here and now noticed at the last moment that the end of the tube was fast approaching the open hatch. She jumped back out of the way as it hit the deck of the landing bay and skidded to the left, away from Quinn and Iov. They sprang for the end, grabbing hold of the controls.

The alien's frustrated roar filled the bay until Liang thought her eardrums would pop. "No! You cannot have them!" The whole station shifted, turning away from the waiting ships. The airlock tube jerked away, heading out the open hatch. Iov was knocked clear, but Benzi Quinn held on like a pit bull.

"Quinn! Let go!" Liang called to him. If he got out past the protective barrier into space, he'd die almost immediately. He turned to look at her, uncomprehending, and she ran to him, barely getting her hands on the edge of the jacket he wore. She yanked him free just before the tube disappeared out the hatch. They tumbled to the deck.

"Sprechan's ass, woman!" Quinn yelled. "Is that it, then? We've missed it?" He pulled away from her and stood, looking like he wanted to hit the nearest hard object. Uri ran to check on his brother.

Liang keyed her communit. "What's happening, Dani?"

"The station's becoming unstable. We're going to try again. You might have to jump. Stand by."

"Jump?" Quinn said. "Is she out of her bloody mind?"

"What's the alternative? If we stay here, we're likely to die anyway. I'd take the chance." Liang got to her feet, moving back into position by the hatch. "Iov, keep an eye on the door for the alien. The last thing we need is him showing up down here."

"Yes, ma'am."

The airlock tube, already extended, wavered in space as the ship maneuvered again to get it in place. *Like threading a moving needle*, Liang thought. This probably was their last chance. It had to work.

Running footsteps caught their attention, and they all sprang into defensive positions. But it turned out to be the doctor, then the two guards, still restrained in electrical cords, followed by Tommy and Nim dragging along a reluctant Delcin, each having a grip on his upper arm.

"The Agent isn't sure that leaving the station is in his best interest," Tommy said. "I explained to him that the accommodations might not be what he's used to."

Quinn snorted in disgust. "Hey, if he don't want to come, I say leave him for the Ancient. Bastards deserve each other."

"Not an option. I think he and my father ought to have a real conversation. Now that we've seen just how powerful Mr. Delcin is. Or isn't, actually. " He pointed toward the hatch. "Watch out!"

While Liang's attention had been focused on Tommy and his prisoner, the airlock had been getting closer, and it now penetrated the hatch, scraping the deck with a horrible metal on metal screech. Quinn went to fasten it on, but it wouldn't hold still long enough.

"Just go!" Liang ordered. She shoved Uri into the tube. The young Muuvo stopped, frozen for a moment, then he used the handholds to scramble deeper inside, toward their own ship and safety. Iov followed, close on his heels.

"Get some coats and a mask," Liang ordered, as Quinn pushed

her ahead of him then stepped onto the moving tube.

"C'mon, Liang. Don't hold up the process. Move it!"

Seeing Uri reach the *Doubtful's* hatch, she hesitated no longer. It was now or never. She ran lightly up the tube, the chill settling into her bones, the machinations of the unstable station throwing them from side to side. Her steps slowed from the horrid cold as she neared the other end, but friendly hands grabbed her and pulled her safely aboard.

Benzi came behind her, then the Agency doctor, who was surprised to find himself at lasergun point when he stepped out. Nim Williams came behind him, helping the security folk take the doctor and the others into custody. He paused for a moment, looking over Liang.

"You're all right?" he asked, the old tenderness in his voice.

"Fine," she said. Her gaze swept the bay deck. Captain Rogers was noticeably absent. Garrett Rawls leaned against the wall, casually supervising. What was going on?

She peered behind her anxiously into the tunnel, where Tommy wrestled with a reluctant Delcin. As she watched, the open hatch faded into invisibility for a moment, then returned. The air was filled with a sharp electrical burnt smell. The airlock slipped dangerously toward the edge of open space.

"Leave him!" she called down the tube. "We're about to lose the station."

Tommy studied her for a split second, obviously torn. He let go of Delcin. "Your choice, pal." He ran up the flexing tunnel, barely staying upright until he reached the hatch, where Liang and Quinn grasped his wrists, pulling him safely aboard.

The station quivered again, and the tube slipped out of the hatch. Delcin stumbled and fell, but stayed inside.

Liang, cognizant of the harm that Delcin had caused her and her crewmates, couldn't ignore her moral compass. "Hurry, Agent Delcin! You have enough air to reach the hatch. If you come now."

"Why don't you reel that old boy in like a big old bass?" Garrett asked with his usual lazy smile. "Not like he's got somewhere else to go."

Dani grinned. "That's an idea." She set the opaque shell to retract mode. The tunnel slowly collapsed at the ship-side end, pulling the open end closer and closer. Delcin, gasping for air, looked desperately at the ship, then out at his precarious proximity to the stars. He was trapped.

"Go ahead and jump," Iov said. "It's what you deserve, after the manner you treated us!"

Liang was shocked. She'd never heard any of the Muuvos utter a threat to anyone. *But everyone has a breaking point. Apparently we've reached his.*

She thought, for a moment, Delcin would take Iov's advice. His gasping, however, got more pronounced, and he eventually crawled up the tunnel to the waiting security officers. He stumbled onto the deck and fell, lying prostrate, his skin white from exposure to the low temperatures.

"I...demand to call...my ship," he wheezed.

Tommy leaned down close to him. "You know what, my friend? On this ship, you don't get to demand anything." He turned to Tabio. "Take them away."

The Agency people were led out. Quinn helped the engineering team secure the tunnel and got the hatch squared away.

"We all set and sound?" Garrett asked.

"Yes, sir," Dani said.

Garrett hit the intercom. "Get us out of here."

"We're gone," Dutton replied, from what Liang assumed was the bridge.

The ship got under way. Nev showed up and a happy reunion took place among the Muuvos, who left the bay to celebrate in private. Nim had gone with security, so Liang stood off to the side, alone for the moment. Tommy took a long look around, focused on Garrett and crossed his arms.

"So what's happened to my father?"

CHAPTER 25

TEMMS lost constant mental contact with Monty during the exchange, the medication Okalani had given him allowing him to drift into sleep every so often. A spike of excitement would bring him back to consciousness, but often into an alarmed state as things appeared to be going wrong. Knowing there was physically nothing he could do, he clung to the threads of the mental conversation, hoping for good news.

He sensed Monty's relief when first Liang, then Benzi came aboard. A rush of activity thereafter confused him, as it seemed like there were more people on the deck than there ought to be, but Monty couldn't sort it out. Finally, there seemed to be a long spate of peace, and Monty's emotions were of success and satisfaction. They'd come home.

All are safe.

Then our time here is concluded. We shall now permanently deactivate the device. We wish you well, Captain Rogers, you and your brave crew. Blessings into the next world.

Knowing the long ordeal was over, Temms quit fighting the urge and let go on the slide into the dark.

Bad dreams plagued him. A clown with a face like Jak Moster mocked him. More teeth, more claws. Tommy lying dead on a field of grass. Kitana lying, burnt, on the damaged bridge of the ship. In another, he was trapped with his ex-wife Connie in an elevator, while she lectured him on all his shortcomings. Finally, the dark was no longer a place of solace, but a place from which to escape.

He fought his way through the fog into the light. Voices were once again around him. He listened for a moment, testing his muscles. His legs felt strong. His heart beat regularly. Breathing didn't hurt as much as it had the last time he was awake. Maybe he would be all right.

You're awake!

Monty's delighted mental voice cheered him.

I AM. EVERYTHING WENT WELL?

Everyone came home safe. My father is here. I am happy.

"G-Good." It took a moment for him to realize he had spoken aloud. Conversation around him fell silent, and then exploded in a cacophony of sound. The room was crowded with people.

"Temms—"

"Captain!"

"Dad! It's about time. What—"

"Let me check him." Okalani came into his field of vision, stopping to listen to his chest with her stethoscope. "Everybody hush!"

Obedient silence fell again, and she hmmed and hawed, very much like her predecessor, dissatisfied with her first readings and her second. Finally she shook her head.

"I'm not sure how you're still alive. But you are." Her eyes teared up, though she was smiling. "Welcome back."

"T-Thanks." Thinking the words wasn't such a struggle, but making his lips form them was. "Tommy?"

"I'm here, Dad." His son stepped into view, a bruise fading under one eye. He looked otherwise unharmed. "The whole team is back safe, including Williams. Liang discovered the Agency had a behavior control chip in him. We snagged a couple of bonus players as well."

Curious, Temms tried to ask a question, but couldn't. His gaze swung around to meet Monty's.

WHAT DOES HE MEAN, BONUS?

Monty studied a puzzled Tommy a moment. *Officers of the Agency are here. Including...Delcin?*

WHERE ARE THEY? HERE? His breath caught and he looked around, awaiting attack.

They are locked in the security section. Monty smiled. *They are not happy about it.*

"Dad?" Tommy asked, brow furrowed.

"Too sick, "Monty said. "He tells me. I tell you. All good."

It interested Temms that aloud, Monty reverted to his old speech, though a direct mind-to-mind connection produced nearly flawless language. Perhaps the direct connection bypassed whatever had been rerouted in his brain that delaying his processing capabilities. Feeling himself wandering off again, he squeezed Okalani's hand, letting her touch bring him back to ground.

"Oh," Tommy said. "I—I—okay."

"You talk. He hears."

"Right." He looked at Temms. "Delcin, his doctor and some others are in the brig below. I don't think the Agency has realized we have them, just yet. I wanted a chance to talk to you before they called anyone. To see if we could negotiate the deal you wanted in exchange for Delcin's freedom."

NOW THE BOY'S THINKING LIKE A MAN. Satisfaction flowed through Temms like warm syrup.

He nodded, noting a pull on his left shoulder at the movement. He glanced down at his left forearm. It was nearly white, his fingers curled tight. He tried to straighten his fingers and realized he had no feeling in that arm at all. None. A sizzle of panic hitting him, he turned to Okalani, studying her intently.

"Arm?" he asked.

She looked away.

He turned to Tommy, who also had an uncomfortable expression on his face.

What was so bad no one could even look at him? He tried to raise himself up in the bed, but Okalani quickly laid a hand on his right shoulder to keep him still.

She looked him in the eye. "Temms, you were attacked by the Kiritan. Do you remember that?"

He nodded once, knowing that's where all the teeth and claws in his dreams came from.

"The animal bit through your shoulder, destroying the clavicle and the rotator cuff. The head of the humerus was also crushed. The claws pierced your rib cage, but fortunately didn't hit your heart." She cleared her throat, took a long breath. "Bacteria in the animal's mouth got into your system, causing a septic shutdown. We've treated with a battery of antibiotics." She traced a triangle over his upper left chest. "You lost skin, tendons and muscle to necrotizing fasciitis."

As she continued to speak, Temms felt each sentence like a punch to the gut. It sounded serious—no, deadly. He remembered Monty's initial contacts, wanting to connect with him before it was "too late."

She hesitated, watching his face. He nodded to encourage her to finish.

"We rebuilt the shoulder the best we could, repairing the damage with artificial bones, and replacing the shoulder ball and socket. Swelling and infection have been the real enemies." She took a shuddering breath. "I don't know if we can save your arm."

He looked down at his wounded fingers again, dismay and disbelief setting in. How would he be able to captain his ship as a crippled man? The last thing he wanted was to put his crew at risk again, in any way.

"Riviera?"

"She came through fine. You took the worst of it, Temms."

MONTY, WHERE ARE WE? IN SPACE, I MEAN? ARE WE STILL OUTSIDE THE STATION?

Monty looked beyond Tommy to someone out of Temms' line of sight. "Captain say where are we?"

Garrett Rawls stepped into view. It took him a moment to sort through his jumbled thoughts and recognize him. He shouldn't be here. He had his own ship to manage.

"I'm glad to see you're awake, pal." He smiled and laid a hand on Temms' left leg. He was infinitely grateful to feel that touch.

AT LEAST I HAVEN'T LOST EVERYTHING.

"We're on the far side of Marriel. The first thing Dutton did once everyone was aboard was hightail it out of there. No one intended to give the alien another shot at controlling you or your people."

"Y-You?" he asked.

"Me? Why am I here?"

"Dutton and I have taken turns helping your very capable staff make decisions in your absence from the bridge. You've certainly stuck your neck out on our behalf often enough. It's the least we could do."

"N-Nik?"

Garrett grinned. "Nikki's got more tricks up her sleeve than I can keep count of. Guess she was able to distract the monster until old Riviera could haul you out of there. She's got some scratches and bumps, but she's okay."

The realization flooded Temms with relief. "Thanks," he whispered.

Tommy coughed discreetly. "Liang wanted to be notified when you were awake. She's been very worried about you."

Temms nodded again, feeling the pull in his bandaged shoulder. Annoyed that even this brief interaction had worn him out, he fought to stay awake, at least until Liang came.

She burst through the door a few minutes later, wan and looking the worse for wear. She skidded to a stop, then made her way through the gathered visitors.

Okalani shooed out several people, Tommy and Garrett among them, leaving Lavan to tend the captain's medical needs, Liang and Monty, in case translation was needed. She stepped out as well, giving the captain some privacy.

Liang took a seat next to the bed, searching his face with her dark gaze. "It is good to see you awake," she said. "How are you feeling?"

"N-not dead y-yet." He tried to manifest a smile.

She didn't seem convinced. "You know men don't go up against the Kiritan."

"Hmmph."

"How can I help you?" She leaned closer. "Is there something you wish to know? Something I can bring?"

So many questions floated, half-formed, in his mind. His fatigue made it hard to hold on to any of them very long. He looked at Monty. *TOP OF THE LIST. THE ANCIENT AND HIS DEVICE. WHERE DO WE STAND?*

Monty passed on the question to Liang.

She raised an eyebrow at Monty's role, but went on smoothly. "Once we had all returned, the device was disintegrated. We thought perhaps you had an explanation."

WISH I DID.

The other voice. The voice from space. The old one. Monty fidgeted at the end of the bed. *When it told us how to construct the machine, it said the machine would have to be eliminated. Permanently this time.*

SO THE ANCIENT HELPING US DESTROYED IT?

Monty nodded. Temms gestured to Liang with his good hand, and Monty shared the details. She sighed with relief.

"We hoped it was something like that. Now that station will never be able to cause harm again." She eyed Temms. "But you trusted another alien with our lives."

"No choice."

She shrugged. "Perhaps. Did they tell you about Nim?"

A host of emotions ran through Temms, remembering his first news of Liang and Nim Williams after they had been taken. He had been prepared to take the man apart for hurting his first officer. But seeing the glow of her face, the clear affection in her eyes, he imagined now that action would hurt her as much as the earlier bruises.

"Chip?"

"Yes. From Sol Aeris." She explained what she'd discovered. "All the graduates we took on that day should be examined for potential sleeper devices."

"Agreed."

He felt his eyes closing of their own accord, and he struggled to keep them open.

Monty patted the captain's good arm. "Captain needs naptime. More questions later."

Liang got to her feet. "One more thing. The Lumina has taken unprecedented action and delayed her ceremony until you are well enough to attend. She told the council that you had singlehandedly saved the quadrant from the potential threat of this station, and she wanted to present you honors personally." She smiled. "Also, it doesn't hurt that her first act of office was to end a serious threat to the Consortium with very little loss of life or expense."

Tears stung his eyes. Singlehandedly? Not hardly. He'd always treasured his independence and the decisions he made on his own. But this endeavor had been concluded only with the sacrifices and hard work of many. Every single one of them, all these family members, deserved any honor he might get. All he could do for now was nod. He'd speak to them later and tell them all, every one, how important they were to him, and how proud he was of their combined effort.

"You rest, sir." Her eyes twinkled with encouragement and caring. "I'll be back when you wake up."

"Love," he said.

Her smile widened. She hesitated, then leaned down to put a soft kiss on his forehead, before she hurried out.

LOVE? THAT WASN'T WHAT I MEANT TO SAY.

Monty grinned. *But it's what you feel. For her. For all. You sleep now. Get well. My sister awaits.*

He scampered out after Liang. Lavan dimmed the lights overhead, and Temms relaxed the best he could into the pillow. Whatever happened now, he'd touched base with his crew, all seemed well. Delcin awaited him in the brig. Certainly he'd have to recover his strength before he confronted that *jumma*'s ass.

BETTER GET STARTED ON THAT.

He let go of his whirling thoughts and slipped into the most restful sleep since he'd returned to the ship.

CHAPTER 26

LIANG personally took Nim to see the doctor, once the initial fuss about dealing with the Captain was cleared after their arrival. He argued with her all the way, but nothing on the face of the nearest star would have kept her small hand from dragging him all the way to the infirmary.

"Honestly, Liang. You've observed me over the past two days. Have you noticed any hint that the Agency still has its hooks in me? I don't think so."

"I didn't think so before we went to the station, either." She stopped just outside the infirmary door, searching his face with her eyes. "I just want to be sure. If you say no, that means you don't trust me. Or maybe that I shouldn't trust you."

He frowned. "You stood right there—"

"While the Agency doctor told me he'd taken care of it. Why should I believe anything those people say?"

She crossed her arms, a little statue of determination. After what she'd gone through on the station, nothing was going to dissuade her from this.

He leaned close and kissed her forehead. "Whatever you want, Liang. I don't want anything to come between us again."

The touch of his lips and the warmth of his tone sent little shivers up her spine. *I could have walked away from him. And what would have happened then?* Better to trust one's instinct, as Roddi always said. "Good. Now, march."

He opened the door and she went in. He came after, both of them quiet out of respect for the captain's recuperation in the back room. Okalani looked up from her work, dark circles under her eyes, but she managed a smile.

"What can I do for you? Looking for a checkup now that you're back?"

"I'd be happy if you'd give me a scan, Okalani," Nim said. "Liang worries that I've still got some kind of Agency bug in me. I want to show her I am one hundred percent loyal again."

She nodded. "Of course. Come on up on the table."

Liang studied the doctor as she performed the scan. Knowing Okalani's feelings as she did, she guessed it must be difficult to have the Captain here, as a patient. *I'm sure no one has received better care. If anyone can pull him through this, she can.*

Liang and Quinn had hypothesized that this Ancient who'd helped their crew might pull out a miracle and heal Temms Rogers, but once the *odahmeen* was destroyed, no one heard the faintest mental touch from it again. Whoever it was had come and gone, once its business was concluded.

Okalani acttivated the screen. "If there's any foreign objects in his body, they'll show up here. Liang, come take a look. Two sets of eyes are better than one."

She complied with the doctor's request, watching over her shoulder as the scan moved from top to bottom. Though she wasn't medically trained, she saw nothing that seemed to be artificially placed. The scanner itself let off no warning bells. When they were finished, Okalani agreed.

"Nothing I can find. I believe he is ready for duty."

Nim sat up and swung himself off the table. "Duty wasn't my main worry." He reached out and pulled Liang into his arms, kissing her deeply. The sudden rush of emotion nearly took her off her feet.

"This is what I wanted to prove," he said softly. "I don't ever want to be without this again."

Okalani smiled ear to ear. "Oh, you two. So romantic." She gathered her instruments and slipped out of the examination area.

"Thank you for not giving up on me," Nim whispered, still close to her ear.

"You are worth it," she whispered back. "I couldn't imagine that you'd purposely hurt me that way. I was grateful to the universe for an alternate explanation."

He kissed her again. "Maybe we could take the rest of the evening and—" Just as he spoke, his comm unit went off. He pulled reluctantly away from her and answered. "Williams here."

Tommy Rogers' voice came across. "I just got notified that you've been cleared for duty by the doctor. Shift begins in five minutes. I expect to see you there."

"Understood. Williams out."

Nim turned to her and sighed. "So much for time together."

She smiled. "We have plenty of time now. Let's take one day at a time, shall we?"

"Of course."

He took another moment for a warm embrace, then left her to report to his shift. Liang stood in the empty place he'd left her, regretting his departure already.

You're acting like a silly teenaged girl, Liang. Stop mooning after the man. You're here to do a job.

But somehow her usual withdrawn attitude of professionalism refused to bow to the leaps of her heart. For the first time in her life, she'd found someone who truly cared for her in the way her father had cared for her mother. Just for herself, not because of the job she could do, or the money she could bring in trade, or her knowledge of a star system. Just her.

She might have protected her heart for all the years that had come before, but she'd finally grown to the point she could allow someone in. It was the best gift she'd ever given herself.

Delighted with her success, Liang walked silently over to peek in on Captain Rogers, who slept in his secluded space, machines beeping around him. This man's kindness had been the key that first told her she could open her heart. She owed him so much.

She closed her eyes and offered up a quick prayer for his swift recovery, then headed for the bridge to check in with Kai. The crew was whole again. Time to get back to business.

CHAPTER 27

FINALLY, the morning came where Temms woke up with a clear head and substantially less pain.

Better take advantage of it while I can. I've got some business that really shouldn't wait.

He grabbed the rail of the infirmary bed with his right hand and hauled himself upright, the sudden movement making his head spin.

His first instinct was to lie back down.

No. No, you don't. You need to get up and get moving. You've got trouble waiting, right here in your security office, and you've got to get it taken care of. Now.

He slid forward until his feet touched the floor, still hanging on to the bedrail. His knees buckled, and he clutched the rail, his arm sliding down to almost his shoulder. His knee bumped the table/tray next to his bed, and it fell over with a large crash.

"What in Sprechan's name are you doing?" Okalani shouted, running into the back room. Her eyes widened as she saw him out of bed. She lunged for him, sliding her shoulder under his right one, helping him stand upright. "You get back to bed this instant."

"I've got to deal with the Agency people."

"Right now?" Disbelief was written on her face like a canonical commandment.

"They're going to figure out what's happened, sooner rather than later. They'll realize we have their Agent and the others. We've got to lay down some rules, an agreement, before then. Give me whatever you have that'll make me look like I'm at full working strength."

She gave him a withering look. "Your left shoulder and arm are practically held together with wire and glue."

He glanced down, seeing it was true. "Well, then, let's hang it in a sling or something. I've got some loose shirts. I need to negotiate a settlement with them. I need Tommy. And Liang."

Okalani pursed her lips, not moving a step. "You're not ready."

"I have to be, 'Lani. We've almost made it through this thing. Come on, help me finish it. Please?"

With a growl, she beckoned to Nev and Lavan, who stood in the doorway, staring. "You heard the captain. Let's get him dressed and get his soldiers ready to march into war with him." She wagged a finger in his face. "But don't you dare complain afterward!"

He smiled and shook his head. "I promise. No complaints. And you can hand me all the 'I told you so' that you want."

"Count on it."

But she smiled as she found him a wheelchair.

The better part of an hour later, he was seated in that chair, dressed, arm in a sling hung awkwardly from the other shoulder, listening to Liang and Tommy as they took turns filling him in on what had happened since they'd left the station. He hadn't missed much. Most important, no one from the Agency had contacted them, looking for their lost boys.

They must suspect we abandoned them on the station. If the Ancient is trapped there, too, perhaps they've given up on getting them back.

Which put Temms in a tenuous place: how could he wring the concessions he wanted from the Agency now?

While he was half-asleep, drifting in and out of consciousness, it had seemed to him that he would be able to somehow use Delcin as a wedge to move the Agency. He hoped that was still possible.

"Has Delcin said anything?" he asked Tommy. "Asked for anyone? Offered any compromise?"

Seated on a desk across from the infirmary bed, Tommy shook his head. "The first couple days he constantly demanded contact with his ship. But he's withdrawn since, sits in the room staring at the wall."

"Is he—" He glanced at Okalani.

"They're all in good health. One of the security people had a banged up elbow when he arrived. But now he's fine. Delcin's mood isn't physical, as far as I can tell," she said.

Temms took in the information, sitting uncomfortably in the chair. He tried to straighten his shoulder, but the movement sent a lightning arrow of pain through his neck and back. He groaned, and Okalani was on him like a starving cat.

"Do you need to put this off? Get back to bed?"

"No," he said firmly.

"Can I give you another shot?"

Tommy snorted with derision. "Right. Because he wants to be a gibbering idiot by the time he interrogates Delcin."

She turned to him, pain in her eyes. "That's not what I—"

Tommy immediately relented, coming off the desk to put a comforting hand on her shoulder. "Lani, I didn't mean it that way. I'm sorry."

A silent exchange passed between them, then she moved away. "I'm just trying to help."

Even in his less than healthy state, Temms was perceptive enough to realize something beyond the ordinary had happened between his son and the doctor. *How long has that been going on? And how didn't I notice it?*

Liang coughed discreetly behind him. "Perhaps we should go. The sooner we finish, the sooner you can rest, sir."

"You're right. I'll go now."

"*We'll* go," she insisted.

"I'm already crippled. If I have to have babysitters to get me through this confrontation, what kind of message will that bring?"

Tommy hunkered down next to the chair, looking his father in the eye. "Let's intend the message to be that you come from a place of strength, with strong people beside you. He knows what we did, getting off the station. It will be the three of us—add one of the Bellonans, if you like, to rub another failure in his face. But he'll be all alone. No staff, no Agency to back him up. It's the worst position he can be in."

"And you are the only man to be attacked by a Kiritan and live," Liang added softly. "What could inspire more respect than that?"

He refrained from pointing out that going into the caves of Lennor wasn't his wisest choice ever, realizing his stamina was beginning to slip away. Now or never.

"Let's do it."

CHAPTER 28

KILE Delcin had been locked in the lower level of the *Doubtful* for days, in a tiny room with pale gray walls, a sink and a toilet. The others were close by, he guessed, but he hadn't been allowed to speak to them. Now he waited. The longer he waited, the more the reality of his situation built like collapsed walls over his head, weighing him down into despair.

Tuon Donn had already told him he was in disgrace, for not meeting his quota for the quarter. Now look at him. Far past disgrace. Much closer to total catastrophe.

Where had he gone wrong?

His intent had been to score a huge jewel in the Agency's crown, this mysterious space station that had been rumored for years. He'd actually negotiated a way inside, welcomed by that miserable, useless Ancient. His people had studied the tech, but acknowledged Rogers' crew was far better versed in the details. So he'd left them to their decoding work.

Mistake number one.

He'd anticipated that these engineers would work hard to complete the job, so they could return to their ship.

Whether I'd have let them go is another point—moot now. It never happened.

For whatever reason, the team appeared to have intentionally botched the decoding process. Nothing of any real use worked until that day, at the end, when they'd left the station. Somehow they'd disrupted the shield long enough to be rescued. If only he'd known that would happen, he could have called his ship, and the *Shelim* would have blasted the thing, demonstrating to this Ancient who was superior. But he'd missed it.

Mistake number two.

Underestimating the *Doubtful* crew was a big one. But despite that, instead of leaving him on the station with his men, Tommy Rogers and the traitor Williams had taken them along when the team made its escape. Why had they done that? He wouldn't have bothered, if the situations had been reversed. He'd have let them die.

So here he was, without the station, without the Bellonans, empty-handed. What could he offer if Tuon Donn showed up right now to negotiate for his release? Nothing. He was finished.

Footsteps came down the hall outside his room, but Delcin ignored them. So many people had come by. No one spoke to him.

But this time they did.

"Hey, Delcin! The Captain wants to see you."

It was Tommy Rogers, his face split with a dazzling grin as he opened the door. He wore a sidearm at his waist. Behind him stood an olive-skinned man in a uniform, whose eyes were a piercing gold, with odd irises. Delcin realized this was one of the Bellonans, in its human form. He stood up slowly, studying the two. "What's he want?"

Tommy kept smiling. "You'll see."

"Are my staff well?"

"They're just fine. Never better." He stepped aside. "Come on, move it."

Surprised they didn't lock him in handcuffs, he walked ahead of the security team along a narrow corridor, and into a lift. They went up one floor, and stepped out, then crossed the hall to the same conference room he'd first visited on the ship. The reception was considerably cooler, with no refreshments, and himself the worse for wear in a dirty uniform that smelled of human misery.

The biggest surprise was his first look at Temms Rogers. He'd expected to find a man capitalizing on his success, practically dancing with joy. The hollow-cheeked man in the wheelchair, his arm wrapped and suspended in a cloth cast, bore resemblance to the captain he'd first encountered only in the ostentatious brightness of his orange-flowered shirt, and the determination in his steely blue eyes.

What in blazes had happened here?

Tommy indicated a chair for Delcin, and he took a seat.

Captain Rogers straightened, a little wince crossing his face. "You'll have to forgive me for not meeting you when you became a guest on my ship. I was otherwise occupied."

Delcin watched Liang, seated next to the captain. Her expression was concerned, and her eyes hardly left the captain's face. Delcin's experience in negotiating told him Rogers was less healthy than he wanted to appear. In other circumstances, he'd have taken the upper hand and crushed the other side.

But these were not other circumstances.

Might as well come on as strong as possible. No telling what the *Doubtful* crew knew. He took a deep breath. "No offense taken, Captain. I do fail to see why we've been held here like prisoners, instead of returned to our ship."

The captain smiled. "Honestly, it's because we have no idea where your ship is. It left the vicinity of the station about twelve days ago and no one's spotted it since."

Delcin's mind spun. The *Shelim* left him? And went where? More importantly, who was commanding it? *It's my ship!*

He bit his lip, trapping his protest inside while he considered a response.

Rogers didn't wait. "I'd thought this would be a good time that you and I could collaborate on a new agreement between the Agency and the mercenary captains. Something a little more reasonable."

That's all he needed, another failure. If the fates were punishing him for some evil he'd done, clearly they weren't finished yet. But he couldn't admit defeat.

"That would depend on what you had to offer, Captain."

"What I have to offer? Hmm." Rogers scribbled on the datapad in front of him and slid it over to Liang. She glanced at it, then at Delcin, then shrugged.

Delcin's foot tapped on the floor, out of his control. His back was straight, hands folded calmly on the table only by sheer force of will. He had nothing to offer in return. He'd be lucky to get command of his ship back when he appeared in the world again, much less have any power to offer concessions.

How different from the last time I sat here. I was so sure of myself then. Now I'm a filthy mess.

"What we need is a flat tariff," Rogers said. "If the cost of doing business in the system is going to be five percent, then we need to know that to figure into our transactions. We'd agree to five percent. No higher."

"But you know we've set the tariffs at twenty. Why would we go to five? Ridiculous."

Rogers just sat and watched him.

Sweat bubbled up on the back of Delcin's neck. His own smell sickened him. Why was Rogers toying with him? "I could speak to Tuon Donn about your outstanding arrest warrant. Perhaps he would quash it in gratitude for the rescue of his men."

"Perhaps?" Rogers chuckled, then winced. Delcin couldn't determine the extent of his injuries, the way he was sitting, but apparently it was pretty bad. Who'd take over if Rogers couldn't run the ship? The petite, silent first officer, or the loud-mouthed son standing behind Delcin? "I simply sent a message. I'm glad it was received."

"I'm not sure what you want me to say, Rogers. I haven't been allowed to contact my ship. I don't even know where it is, or—"

"Or where you stand?"

The confidence with which the question was asked clued Delcin that while Rogers' body might be ailing, his mind was plenty sharp.

"I'm sorry?" he asked, hoping he'd misheard.

"My crew has reported to me the general tone of conversation between you and Donn, and you and the Ancient. It sounded to them like you were on your way out, unless you could produce something that mattered for the Agency. Unfortunate that the acquisition of the station didn't work out like you'd anticipated, so that was the first failure. Then I hadn't yet had time to discuss your request for one of the Bellonan offspring, or the mated pair, with my officer. Tabio? Would you like to weigh in on that?"

A sibilant hiss and a growl came from behind Delcin, the combination sending an icicle of fear melting down his spine.

"I would kill him before he touched me or mine," Tabio said.

Rogers nodded and tapped his datapad. "So there's your answer. It looks like you've got no value to the Agency at the moment. Trying to negotiate an agreement with you seems like a waste of your time and mine." He studied Delcin. "So what shall I do with you? Turn you back over to them, a defeated man? Or do you have another suggestion?"

Delcin wanted to argue. But he stumbled over Rogers' cuttingly blunt logic. What would he do if he returned to the Agency? He'd be demoted, certainly. He'd lose his fancy ship and his title. Donn would give him the chance to work his way back up through the ranks, wouldn't he?

It depends on how far he sends you down. You know he likes to puncture those with hubris, and lay them low. Maybe you'd be reassigned to some menial position and never given the chance to better yourself. The thought made him physically ill.

"We could set you and your men down on Terza or Marriel,"

Rogers added more gently, "so you could have your ship retrieve you. Or you could slip away into the populace and start over."

Start over? After all he'd sacrificed?

No. It wasn't his way. He'd return and face Tuon Donn, even with the likelihood he'd be publicly humiliated. Running away meant he'd never win his place back. However, once back in his own milieu, he knew how to work the system. He'd made plenty of shortcuts in his rise to the top. It just depended on who you knew and what you were willing to do for them.

He cleared his throat.

"If you'd leave us on Terza, an Agency ship will come by for us. That will be adequate."

Rogers' face brightened, as if he hadn't expected that answer. "Consider it done." He turned to Liang. "Make sure the men have a chance to clean themselves up, and issue them a change of clothing. We wouldn't want the Agency to see their officers poorly treated."

"Yes, sir."

She got to her feet. Delcin sensed the meeting had concluded. He just couldn't bring himself to thank Rogers for the outcome. "I'm sure we'll meet again, Captain. Under better circumstances."

Rogers grinned. "I'll look forward to it. Good luck, Delcin. You'll need it."

The Captain nodded to the security officers and they marched Delcin back down the hall to his room. The cheerful way Rogers had wished him luck burned in his mind. He didn't need luck. He had skills. He'd be back.

And if—when—I'm back on top, Rogers just better watch himself. Because a dog you've beaten returns twice as vicious the next time.

CHAPTER 29

TEMMS didn't walk into the ceremony, but he certainly felt ten feet tall as he rode in a wheelchair, a procession of crew members following him in full dress uniform. The faces in the crowd that saw him pass lit with vague recognition, and several of the uniformed attendees stopped talking to incline their head briefly in his direction.

It had been nearly eight weeks since the Kiritan had changed his life forever.

His arm had been saved, but it was no longer functional. For this event, he wore a sling, finding it more dignified than having it dangle uselessly beside him. Okalani had insisted on the chair. He hadn't argued because he needed to maintain a whole day's worth of stamina. The more energy he could save, the longer he would last. With the skies clear, the temperature warm, and the celebration to come, he wanted to drink every drop of the day ahead.

One of the Consortium princes approached the parade, resplendent in white uniform and a deep blue cape lined in gold. Liang, pushing his chair, came to a stop.

"Captain Rogers?"

"At your service," he replied.

"Tisley Grecan," the prince said with a small bow. "My niece has been most complimentary to the boon you have done us all. I wanted to express my appreciation personally." He handed Temms an envelope.

"What's this?" Temms froze, frustrated by his one hand. Opening an envelope that way wasn't easy.

"A small token, Captain, a token only. Along with a letter of conduct in the event you need to traverse the space over Perpetra. You need only give my name and a copy of this certificate, and you will be welcome where you choose to go."

That was no token at all, that was an amazing gift. He heard the crew whispering behind him. "We're grateful, your Highness. Thank you."

"We're glad to have you among us. Best wishes for continued

recovery."

The prince smiled at the rest of the entourage, then moved on.

Tommy leaned down and spoke close to his father's ear. "Let the Agency bite on that!"

Temms chuckled. "I think the Agency has quite enough to deal with without worrying about my free ticket to Consortium space."

A laugh came from behind them. "Well, if it isn't the famed Destroyer of Worlds and now, all-around Hero of the hour."

Temms turned the chair around to face his accoster. "C.T., how are you?"

The two men shook hands warmly.

C.T.'s beautiful companion Kyndra came to stand next to him, draped in folds of terra cotta colored silks and a long woven vest specked with gold beads. She studied Temms for a long moment, then nodded. "You seem much better. Up here." She tapped his forehead.

"I'm doing well. Thank you. I see you're taking good care of my friend."

She feigned a pout. "He only needs so much looking after because of his choice of dangerous friends."

"Oh, I see. He takes no responsibility for any of his adventures." Temms nodded. "Quite the lucky man."

C.T. squeezed Kyndra's arm. "Very lucky. And I know how to quit when I'm ahead."

Liang leaned over Temms' shoulder. "Captain, we need to keep moving or we shall be late."

"Of course, Liang, of course. Please proceed."

C.T. and Kyndra joined the group that included the entire *Doubtful* bridge crew as well as the Bellonans and their young. Rey walked beside his father, trying valiantly to keep up, while the new baby, Chandi, rode atop Aronka's shoulder. They'd told Temms earlier, with great excitement, that the Lumina had given them permission to visit the herd farm, despite her grandfather's edict.

"Who's flying the ship?" C.T. asked.

"No one," Temms replied. "We've landed outside the city for a few days. The air was getting a little rank. Engineering has had an opportunity to make some repairs. Frankly, we've taken advantage of the down time."

"Looks like most of the group is here."

He nodded. "After the incident, the Lumina extended the

invitation to the entire crew. Many of them had never been to Perpetra, to explore the Consortium's head city, so they're waiting to meet us."

"Good. They worked hard while you were lying around." C.T. winked.

Temms chuckled. "Right. That 'vacation' I took."

"Captain!"

Ahead of them, Monty stood at the corner and waved. Benzi Quinn came out a shop just behind him, followed by Zandra Cilka. She leaned close to Benzi's ear and whispered as the Captain's entourage caught up to them. They both seemed thoroughly content, sharing relaxed smiles and a brief, reassuring touch.

"Chief," Temms said in acknowledgement as they approached the three.

"Cap." Benzi grinned. "Pretty snazzy digs around this place. Think I could get used to it."

"I doubt it. You're a spaceman through and through. You wouldn't feel right without a deck humming under your feet and a greasy part to repair in your hand."

"Mayhap you're right, Cap. Don't forget the pretty girls working alongside."

Zandra blushed and Monty clapped his hands. "Happy is good!" he declared.

"Happy is good," Temms agreed.

They entered the plaza where the ceremony was to take place. A section down front had been reserved for the *Doubtful* crew, as well as representatives from each of the ships in the mercenary alliance. The twins Hocai and Pinsan were there already, as were Garrett Rawls, with Valeni and Nikki, both women flamboyantly dressed in bright colors. Tommy and Nim escorted the Captain and his party down the aisle, making sure everyone was seated before sitting along the aisle themselves.

Temms turned to speak to Liang, just as she sidled out of her seat and moved down several chairs to slide in next to Nim. Momentary disappointment turned into paternal pride. *I see my little chick is preparing to leave the nest. After all that girl's been through, I can be nothing but happy for her.*

He surveyed the stage before him, polished wood stretching into violet-curtained backdrop, a solid dark wood podium set toward the front. Two rows of upholstered chairs sat behind the podium. While it looked open to the crowd, he had no doubt, knowing the precision of Consortium security, that it was fully guarded and likely shielded as well. Not that his own security team would let anything happen to their former charge.

Half-expecting Monty to join his sister on the stage, he was just as pleased to find the boy in hot conversation with his adopted father and Zandra. He'd promised Monty he'd bring his father home, and it had been done. The fact that the boy himself had a hand in it made the event even more gratifying. The kid would be one hell of a fine engineer one day. He had the perfect mentor to make sure that took place.

The other captains and members of the crews filled in the seats as the time came to begin the ceremony. Trumpets sounded a fanfare, and the crowd fell silent. A flare of startling blue fireworks went off over head, easily seen even in broad daylight.

"Ladies and gentlemen, princes and commoners, invited guests, welcome! I give you our Lumina, the Honored One. Please rise for her entrance."

The young woman walked onto the stage, trailed by several older men in violet dress uniforms and an assortment of younger men and women in formal dress. In contrast, she appeared in all white, a dress trimmed in something reflective, so that when she hit the sunlight, it cleverly appeared that she was illuminated.

She stopped at the podium, surveying the crowd before her. Temms estimated there had to be two thousand or more gathered for the occasion, most of them Consortium notables if the profusion of liveried servants and fine hats meant anything. He was gratified that she turned a special smile on him just before she began to speak.

"Honored guests, welcome to this, a great day for all subjects of the Consortium. A new Lumina comes to your house only once in a lifetime, and I am indeed honored to be selected for this position. This seat conveys with it an enormous amount of power, and I appreciate your trust in letting me wield it for your benefit.

"And yet even as we carry on with our traditions, we see that others continue to challenge them. I'm not referring to our ongoing rivalry with the Agency, of which you are well aware, but the recent threat of the Genarius, an ancient trouble that we believed long buried. We had allowed ourselves to become complacent.

"Yet one among us faced this danger, and saved us all, as I am sure you've heard by now. Captain Temms Rogers of the ship

Doubtful."

She paused and indicated Temms to the crowd, which murmured and whispered in a wave that surged past the captain and his crew.

"When he came to me with his request for assistance and offer to help, I realized that our previous ways might not always serve our best interest. We have been isolationist for too long. While some would argue that this policy protects us, I believe that it opens us to hidden threats more easily discovered by open communication and commerce."

C.T. leaned forward from his seat behind Temms. "Now you've gone and done it. Those Consortium *paters* are going to need a new set of pants."

Temms chuckled. "She's a spirited girl, I'll give her that."

The young woman's voice rang strong with conviction. "It is hereby decreed that all of the Genarius artifacts are hereby banned. They shall be collected and destroyed so that we will never be held hostage by them again."

Temms briefly considered this proclamation with regret, knowing the destruction of the artifacts would pretty much preclude a return to his own universe forever. He glanced over to Garrett, a man in a similar situation, who only nodded and tipped his wide-brimmed hat. So be it. If he was here to stay, it was not such a bad place to be.

The Lumina continued her speech, replete with the usual reassurances and chauvinistic proclamations. Temms let her voice fade into a gentle buzz in the back of his head, focusing instead on the breaths of impossibly-fresh air that he took, in and out, in a body that was still healing. He savored the sun on his skin, taking in its golden energy. The presence of his crew, finally past the suffering of separation and stress, now reunited with those they cared about, strengthened him. So much he had to be thankful for, and he hoped he could be grateful enough.

Once the formalities were over, the attendees adjourned to a huge banquet hall, where they were served a delightful feast, with course after course of exotically-seasoned dishes. At first self-conscious and leery of his one-armed status at such a function, Temms found that his plate was served with everything already cut to be bite-sized. *That girl thinks of everything. Maybe it's not so bad having her in charge.*

As the guests were finishing their sumptuous fruit custard desserts, the Lumina called everyone's attention to the head table.

"Ladies and gentlemen, I trust you are enjoying your time in the capital. I must say I am honored to have so many of you take time from your schedules to share this day with me. There are just two more matters I wanted to address."

Temms saw Jahn jump up behind the Lumina, as if he were prepared to shush her. Prince Arlen's face flushed red, too.

I wonder what she's trying to do now. Something inappropriate, apparently.

He turned to Liang, seated on his right. "What do you think she's up to?"

Liang studied the scene. "Perhaps she's prepared a statement on the Bellonans."

"Hmm. That might be." And it would certainly explain the reaction.

The Lumina turned and shot a look at Jahn who froze, then sat back in his chair. She then faced the crowd with a bright smile.

"As some of you know, it is tradition for one such as myself, one half of a set of twins born to a ruling family, to be chosen for this particular honor. What I discovered in recent days is what happens to the other half of the twin pair."

She turned wounded eyes on her grandparents.

"How all of you could have allowed this injustice for so many years, where the other twin is just sucked dry and discarded. It shames me."

Prince Arlen stood. Then sat down again and hung his head. The room was silent as a burial mound.

"Fortunately, through the good fortune of my connection with Captain Rogers, I was able to find and meet my other half, a part of my life that's been missing since I was a child." She gestured to the table where Monty sat with Benzi Quinn and the others. "Bena, stand up so everyone can see you."

At first the boy hid his head, too shy to comply, but his companions urged him to stand up and wave, and he finally did. Then a buzz went through the crowd.

"Let me tell you about my brother. He may not be as physically beautiful as I am, but that is not his fault. He has other gifts, what was left to him by those who passed me so many of his good attributes. He engineered the device that rescued both Agency and civilian personnel from the Genarius station. Sweet and loving and kind, despite how poorly he was treated by our own people, I am proud he is my brother."

She pulled out a rolled paper from under her table.

"I'm now signing a law into effect that prevents this atrocity from ever happening again. If twins are born into this universe when it is their time to rule, then they shall rule together, putting all their gifts to work jointly, hand in hand."

She cleared a place in front of her and started to write on the document, despite several men's voices who called from the audience in protest.

"Arlen, do something! The girl has scarcely been in office half a day, and she's determined to turn our whole government upside down!"

"Tradition!" "This can't be done!"

No one at the head table moved, or spoke, or interfered. Temms realized for the first time that those seated with her were not the stodgy old bureaucrats he'd always dealt with, but a cadre of younger, more cheerful men, and women, too. Had she replaced her entire group of advisors? She finished writing, and handed the scroll to Jahn.

Temms, amazed at first, wished he could clap his hands in approval, but instead, he slapped his knee with his good hand, making much the same noise. His companions followed suit, and soon the room resounded with the sound of applause. Monty, excited by all the attention, ducked back into his seat and covered his ears.

"While it is customary for the newly chosen leader to distribute honors to the members of her household at this time, as many of you know, I did so in a private ceremony several weeks ago when the ascension was originally scheduled. All that is left to me tonight is one final gesture of thanks, for Captain Rogers and his crew, who have always treated me with the exact respect I deserved and the honesty I needed. They have put their lives in danger for me and for all of us, and in gratitude I gift to them a new Varker class ship to let them expand their business and flourish, as well as the goodwill of the Consortium and its allies." She lifted her glass. "May good winds and fortune follow them!"

The toast was repeated, glasses clinked, and Temms tried not to choke with the emotions that closed his throat. "Thank you, my Lady, on behalf of all of us," he called out when he could speak. "We are grateful to serve."

That was all he could manage, but it was enough. The triumphant Lumina, looking radiant, invited those in attendance to feel free to walk around the palace grounds, then took her seat again, chatting eagerly with those around her, who clearly congratulated what she'd done.

"Well, if she hasn't stirred the pot now," he said. "What next?"

"What next indeed?" Liang's dark eyes sparkled. "And who's going to captain your new ship?"

Across the table from them, Okalani's eyes widened in surprise. "Why wouldn't he do it himself?"

Tommy leaned forward and grinned. "All right, then who's going to captain the *Doubtful?*"

"Surely not you," Liang said to Tommy. "You've never even sat a bridge shift!"

"You're not even old enough to vote, back home," Tommy shot back.

"What about your temper?"

"And what about your boyfriend?"

"Children!" Temms said firmly. "Let me get used to having a fleet of ships before you all start taking them away from me, will you?"

Dutton passed by, on his way out, and patted Temms on his good shoulder. "Looks like your young friend is shaking up more lives than her own here."

"Tell me about it." He sighed with mock irritation. The last thing he needed, especially when they'd just been honored by the new leader, was a "dad-always-liked-you-best" battle. He saw Tommy and Liang were both waiting for an answer.

"The one thing I'm fortunate to have is a crew that can handle anything, and good friends that can help me accomplish whatever task we set our minds to. I think we'll have plenty to do, getting a new ship ready, whoever eventually flies her."

Benzi Quinn stood up and smiled. "Y'know, rather than have your favorites fight this out and hurt themselves, I'd be glad to take that extra ship off your hands. Just as a personal favor to you, Cap."

Tommy, Liang, Dani, and Temms all said "No!" at the exact same moment.

That sparked laughter and more celebration at the table by the *Doubtful* crew and friends, even though many of the Consortium members began filing out. Temms didn't want to call it a night until later in the evening. After the last two months his team had endured, they deserved a party.

Kyndra came by the table some time later, and asked if she could steal him away for awhile.

"I could use a break from the noise," he said, and allowed her to wheel him outside and along a landscaped walk lined with fragrant white flowers. While the walk was lit, the lights hung low so as not to obscure the stars. It was a lovely view. Temms could have stayed there for hours.

Coming to a small wrought metal table, she stopped, and took a seat, pulling him close so they sat knee to knee. "Tell me, my friend, are you as well as you seem?" she asked, taking his hand. "Or are you putting on a good front?"

He squeezed her fingers. "I must confess I'm tired after the day. But I feel better each day, and gain some strength back. Who knows whether I'll be what I once was?"

"You will always be that, Temms. An honorable man who puts the needs of others before himself, who loves his crew like they were family? Forever, you will be that. Your physical body?" She shrugged. "We all change as we grow old, in different ways."

"I suppose that's true."

"Of course it is. I always give good advice." She laughed softly.

"So, two ships. I might really be in business one of these days, like C.T.." He laughed dryly. "Wait until the Agency hears I have a 'fleet' now. They'll be after me for double tariffs."

His mercenary alliance had been informed of the disposition of Delcin and his staff, with the sad corollary that no serendipitous settlement had gone along with Delcin's release, as they'd all hoped. But on the other hand, the Agency hadn't been obvious in any part of this particular star system since the alien had chased them off the station. Perhaps they were finding their efforts better spent in another part of the sector.

"I'm sure when they're ready, they'll be back," Kyndra said. "No one of their nature walks away from profit." She let go and patted his knee. "I'm sure we'll be ready for them when they return."

"I pray it's so." He leaned back and studied the sky. "It's a strange life we lead."

"Strange but wonderful. So many opportunities out there among the stars. And friends to meet."

"A salute to friends." He raised an imaginary glass, smiling at her.

"A salute to your new dynasty, Temms. Your ships, your son, your daughter." She waved a finger at his beginning objection. "I know she's not of your blood, but you two are clearly dear to each other, like any other parent and child. You are all lucky to have each other."

She stood and leaned close to hug him.

"Here, let me take you back. We'll have a drink to make merry, and I'll watch your crew battle out who gets your ship." She winked, teasing him, and started pushing him back up the walk to the banquet hall.

"I'll definitely need a drink before that starts. Maybe a few. And you might have to bail us all out of jail in the morning."

"Any time for you, Temms Rogers. Any time."

THE END

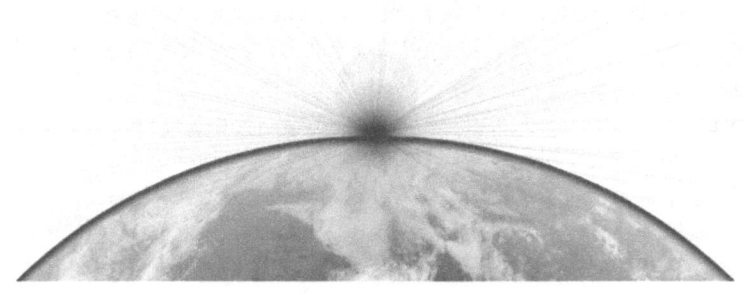

AUTHOR

Lyndi Alexander dreamed for many years of being a spaceship captain, but realized reluctantly that she had been born much too soon. Instead she settles for flights of fancy, inspired excursions into fictional places with fascinating companions from her imagination that she likes to share with others. She has been a published writer for over thirty years, including seven years as a reporter and editor at a newspaper in Homestead, Florida, and her list of publications is eclectic, from science fiction to romance to horror, from tech reporting to television reviews. Lyndi is single mom to a teenager on the autism spectrum, and volunteers at her local domestic violence shelter and for Project Linus.

PUBLICATIONS INCLUDE:

Clan Elves of the Bitterroot urban fantasy series:
THE ELF QUEEN (Book I)
THE ELF CHILD (Book II)
THE ELF MAGE (Book III)
THE ELF GUARDIAN (Book IV)

Horizon Crossover science fiction series:
HORIZON SHIFT (Book I)
HORIZON STRIFE (Book II)
HORIZON DYNASTY (Book III)

Science Fiction novels:
TRIAD

SPECIAL TERMS

ON THE SHIP *DOUBTFUL*:
Temms Rogers: Captain
Kai Windthorp: helm officer
Dani Jamar (D): chief engineer
Liang Chao Chen: *Doubtful* navigator, now first officer
Riviera Brown: junior tactical officer; becomes science officer
Thomas (Tommy) Rogers: captain's son; becomes chief of security
Tasiq: communications officer
Benzi Quinn: engineer assistant with the title of Chief
Okalani Boro: runaway bride; ship's doctor
Lavan: medical orderly
Iov: Muuvo who has joined with his brothers, engineering staff
Nev: Iov's brother, works in medical
Uri: Iov's brother, works in engineering
Zandra Cilka: recruited from the Sol Aeris school, sciences officer
Shiro Vered: sciences officer, often cross-assigned to medical
Gretta Flan: communications officer from Sol Aeris
Nim Williams: security officer from Sol Aeris

ON MARRIEL:
Oke Runyon: saloon owner
Kevan Ankho: Liang's former captain on the *Palva*

ON ROANDOCK:
Jowalt Edward: merchant/parts dealer

ON SOL AERIS TECHNICAL SCHOOL:
Mosk: personnel officer

ON LENNOR:
Rez, Malka, Zareb, Jonel and Karn: Lenci priests and officials Old
  priestess and her helpers

ON TERSA (Home of the Consortium):

Rabal Klin: minister

Hace: minor functionary

The Boy: Abandoned by the Olesians on the ship; taken on by Quinn like a son (Monty)

ON PERPETRA:

The Lumina: young girl in training for her eventual rulership

Prince Arlen: grandfather of the Lumina, important man in both Cartesian culture and economic structure

Aronka and Tabio: shape-shifting security guards of the Bellonan species whotransfer to the *Doubtful*

MERCENARY CAPTAINS ALLIANCE:

C.T. Dutton: long-time associate and friend of Temms, flies the *Fuego*; has an empath as a partner, Kyndra Vilsin

Garrett Rawls: Captain of the *Six-Shooter*, was pulled across the universal divide in a similar way to Temms Rogers, only from Earth. He's picked up two crew, Valeni Pascual and Nikki/ Nicholas, a shape-shifter who can change gender forms.

Lin Hocai and Xi Pinsan: a young sister and brother who fly together, dressed alike, as if they're twins. Dress in Asian style, light silk jackets and tight black pants. Had been trained up into the Agency, but rejected it and went out on their own.

OTHERS:

Kile Delcin: Agency Officer

Tuon Donn: Agency Commander in Chief

Rodolphus (Roddi) : Liang's former instructor

VOCABULARY WORDS:

Lok cha: Deadly drug

Kiritan cave dwellers on Lennor: fierce feline predators

Sprechan: a deity of sorts

Abril: a card game

Odahmeen: a device of the Ancients that has been separated from their invisible station, preventing it from activating to a higher level

Jumma: a large bovine animal

Genarius: the Consortium's word for the Ancients

www.ingramcontent.com/pod-product-compliance
Lightning Source LLC
Chambersburg PA
CBHW022120170626
46808CB00002B/781